Manek Mischiefs

Of Patriarchs, Playboys and Paramours

Lee Su Kim

Marshall Cavendish
Editions

© 2017 Marshall Cavendish International (Asia) Private Limited
Text and photos © Lee Su Kim

Published by Marshall Cavendish Editions
An imprint of Marshall Cavendish International

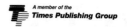

The publisher makes no representation or warranties with respect to the contents of this book, and specifically disclaims any implied warranties or merchantability or fitness for any particular purpose, and shall in no event be liable for any loss of profit or any other commercial damage, including but not limited to special, incidental, consequential, or other damages.

Other Marshall Cavendish Offices:
Marshall Cavendish Corporation. 99 White Plains Road, Tarrytown NY 10591-9001, USA • Marshall Cavendish International (Thailand) Co Ltd. 253 Asoke, 12th Flr, Sukhumvit 21 Road, Klongtoey Nua, Wattana, Bangkok 10110, Thailand • Marshall Cavendish (Malaysia) Sdn Bhd, Times Subang, Lot 46, Subang Hi-Tech Industrial Park, Batu Tiga, 40000 Shah Alam, Selangor Darul Ehsan, Malaysia

Marshall Cavendish is a registered trademark of Times Publishing Limited

National Library Board, Singapore Cataloguing-in-Publication Data

Name(s): Lee, Su Kim.
Title: Manek mischiefs : of patriarchs, playboys and paramours / Lee Su Kim.
Description: Singapore : Marshall Cavendish Editions, [2017]
Identifier(s): OCN 974932248 | ISBN 978-981-47-7178-8 (paperback)
Subject(s): LCSH: Peranakan (Asian people)--Fiction.
Classification: DDC M823--dc23

Printed in Singapore by Markono Print Media Pte Ltd

Dedicated to

Stephen J Hall
and Lee Jan Ming
with love

and to the memory of my parents,
Mr and Mrs Lee Koon Liang

Contents

Preface

Manek Mischiefs completes the trilogy of stories of the unusual and unique Peranakan community.

After writing two collections of short stories, *Kebaya Tales* and *Sarong Secrets*, I thought the series was completed, only to be coaxed and cajoled to write another collection. I decided to take up the challenge, this time focusing on the stories of the babas. Just as *Kebaya Tales* was inspired by my mother's stories, this book is inspired by a baba I loved very much and still do. He was my father, Mr Lee Koon Liang, a baba from Malacca who could not speak a word of Chinese but had an excellent command of English and Baba Malay. He was a wonderful and loving father, a man of integrity and courage with a great sense of humour. Unlike my mother, he was a man of few words, but when he spoke, his words always meant a lot. He enjoyed taking photos with his Brownie camera. I asked my Pa once why he took so many photos and his reply was, "To be remembered." One of these photos I remember well is of my mother in her sarong kebaya and her favourite pair of kasut manek.

The word manek ('beads' in Malay) is used to describe the minuscule glass beads from Bohemia and Czechoslovakia, brought over to this region by traders. In the past, beaded shoes or kasut manek and beaded items with intricate designs were made solely for weddings and for ornamental purposes. From the mid-19th century onwards, wealthy baba families tried to ensure their nyonya daughters were skilled in the domestic arts including beading and embroidery in order to become good wives and homemakers. A test of a well brought-up nyonya was her skill and patience reflected in the refinement and creativity of the beadwork items she made for the prenuptial exchange of gifts ceremony. Beaded items included kasut manek slippers for the bridegroom, pillow and bolster ends, decorations for the bridal bed, table mats and runners, covers for tables, mirrors, beds and footstools, cases for watches, magnifying glasses and spectacles, boxes for hairpins or jewellery, panels for door and window lintels and many more.

I grew up in an extended family setting and remember a home full of delicious, spicy and piquant aromas as my nyonya mother loved to cook, but do not remember either Grandma or my mother ever doing any kind of embroidery or beading. They told me they just did not have the patience or the inclination. However, watching them dress up for a formal event in their elegant sarong kebayas always meant watching them slip on, as the final touch, those gorgeous, colourful kasut manek, a necessary accessory to complete their graceful outfits. I have decided to name this book after the vibrant and brilliantly-coloured manek, the last book in this collection of stories about a beautiful heritage culture and community. It has been a wonderful journey through the images and words involving sarongs, kebayas and now manek. I have learnt a lot and enjoyed writing these stories. I'm pleased this trilogy is complete.

Lee Su Kim
February 2017

Acknowledgements

I'd like to thank my uncles, babas Foo Yat Kee and Foo Yat Chin for sharing their experiences of the Japanese occupation of Malaya. My thanks to Alan Maley who showed great interest in my stories and provided valuable feedback. To the many friends who assisted: Sim Chandler, Phaik See and Chin Lim who shared real-life stories from Penang, Lina Lim who provided valuable ideas for stories when I was feeling exhausted and dry of ideas, Kelly for sharing her story, babas Lee Yuen Thein and David Neo and Ms Tan Siew Imm who provided assistance in baba idioms and expressions, my sister Su Win who helped remember some details of childhood days, my brother Yu Ban who read the draft of my last story with such calm when I was in turmoil and all the kind friends and acquaintances who have encouraged me to continue writing. To a dear friend, Harriet Wong, thank you for your encouragement and steadfast support. To Baba Chan Eng Thai, thank you for the pantun.

I am deeply indebted to Ken Yap who generously availed to me photographs of items from his collection of Peranakan artefacts, including exquisite manek items. A big thank you to Cheah Hwei-Fe'n, author of *Phoenix Rising: Narratives in Nyonya Beadwork from the Straits Settlements*, for your kind assistance. I'd like to thank Jackie Yoong, curator of The Peranakan Museum, for your interest in my book and assistance, and the Peranakan Museum of Singapore for allowing me to feature several items from the museum. My gratitude extends to Mr and Mrs Tye Soon Ping for allowing me to photograph items from their kasut manek collection. My thanks go to baba Peter Wee of Katong Antique House, Singapore and author of *A Peranakan Legacy: The Heritage of the Straits Chinese* for his kind assistance. My thanks also go to baba Peter Lee, author of *Sarong Kebaya: Peranakan Fashion in an Interconnected World* for his inspiring work and words.

I've enjoyed working with the team at MCIA: thank you Lee Mei Lin and She-reen Wong for being such a pleasure to work with. To Violet Oon, thank you for getting me started on this trilogy and Leslie Lim who hinted a long time ago. My thanks go to my son, Lee Jan Ming, for taking many of the photographs in this book and for your interest in my stories. Finally, thank you dearest Stephen Hall for reading every word, for your encouragement, ideas and guidance and for all the time you've given me. It's your love and keen appreciation of my culture and heritage that sustain and inspire me in my writing endeavours.

About the Babas and Nyonyas

Origins

The babas and nyonyas of Malaysia and Singapore are a unique ethnic group which originated 700 years ago when Chinese traders arrived in Malacca, the centre of the Malacca Sultanate. The traders sojourned in Malacca for around six months, waiting for the monsoons to change direction and take them home to Fujian, on China's southeastern coast. They did not bring their womenfolk along and many intermarried with the local women. It was from these crosscultural unions that the babas and nyonyas evolved. Intermarriage between the babas and the local women eventually ceased, and for hundreds of years past, the babas married exclusively amongst their own people, becoming an endogamous and elite group.

Another interesting theory as to the origins of the babas and nyonyas is the legend of the Chinese princess, Hang Li Po, sent to marry the Sultan of Malacca to boost diplomatic ties between Malacca and China. The *Malay Annals* describes vividly the arrival of the Chinese princess Hang Li Po in Malacca with an entourage of five hundred ladies and courtiers. The princess and her retinue settled down at a place called Bukit China. The Sultan of Malacca, Sultan Mansur Shah, ordered a well dug at the foot of Bukit China for his Chinese bride. Both the well, Perigi Hang Li Po, and Bukit China are still in existence in Malacca today.

The babas and nyonyas are also known as the Peranakan, the Straits Chinese and Straits-born Chinese. The word 'Peranakan' is derived from the Malay word '*anak*' which means 'child'. The term refers to local-born as well as the offspring of foreigner-native union. Baba is an honorific from northern India for 'man', nyonya is an honorific for 'woman' in Malay adopted from the Portuguese word for grandmother.

Culture

The Baba nyonya culture is a rare and beautiful blend of many cultures – Chinese and Malay, mixed with elements from Javanese, Sumatran, Thai, Burmese, Balinese, Indian, Portuguese, Dutch and English cultures. The influence of European elements was because Malacca was conquered by three colonial powers successively: the Portuguese in 1511, the Dutch in 1641 and the British in 1825.

The culture is very much localised in essence, and proudly Chinese in form. The babas kept to their patriarchal culture, with male offsprings bearing the family name, while the mother culture was maintained by the womenfolk. In Malacca and Singapore, the Peranakan spoke Baba Malay, a patois of the Malay language with many loan words from

Hokkien and English. In Penang, Hokkien was spoken instead of Baba Malay. The customs were heavily Chinese in form, as the babas and nyonyas clung loyally to their Chinese identity. Filial piety was very important and ancestral worship was core to the culture.

The lifestyle of the nyonyas was a unique balance between Chinese and Malay world traditions. The traditional nyonya costume was the *baju panjang* which can be traced to Javanese origins. It consisted of a long, loose calf-length top with long sleeves worn over a batik sarong. The collar is Chinese and the dress is fastened by a set of *kerosang* (three brooches linked by a gold chain).

By the end of the 1920s, young nyonyas abandoned the austere *baju panjang* for the more attractive nyonya kebaya. The short kebaya was more flattering and shapely, with intricate embroidery at the neckline, sleeves and hem. Nyonyas preferred the Pekalongan batik sarongs from Java because of their vibrant colours and motifs of birds, flowers and animals.

Nyonya food is a wonderful combination of Malay and Chinese cuisine with Southeast Asian and European influences. Using a variety of ingredients and cooking methods, herbs and spices and occasionally, Western influences such as Worcester sauce, the nyonyas concocted a unique cuisine – the original fusion food with predominantly hot, spicy and piquant flavours. Peranakan cuisine is labour intensive and considered an art. Condiments are important on the nyonya's dining table especially the ubiquitous *sambal belachan*. A nyonya's cooking ability could be assessed, in the olden days, from the rhythms of the way she pounded the *sambal belachan*.

The babas and nyonyas today

Today, the baba and nyonya community still survives with its strongholds in Malacca, Penang and Singapore. Many younger generations of Peranakan have moved to live and work in Kuala Lumpur. (There are also Peranakan communities in Kelantan and Terengganu on the east coast of Peninsular Malaysia; Phuket, Thailand; Indonesia; Myanmar; Laos and Vietnam.) With globalisation and further migration, the Peranakans have settled all over the world with large communities in Melbourne, Sydney, Perth and London.

Both the old historic Quarters of Georgetown and Malacca, where Peranakan enclaves are located with its unique architecture and lifestyles, were declared World Heritage Sites by UNESCO in 2009.

PANTUN SATU KERETAR DUA LEMBU

Bungah Rose harum wangi,
Kerumun banyak tabuan lebar,
Carik perompuan siang pagi,
Gila urat betol si Inche Baba!

Dalam rumah laki kita,
Bila luar jangan cemburu,
Perkara ini orang kata
Satu keretar dua lembu!

Sweet smelling is the rose,
Bees & wasps surround it,
Day & night chasing skirts,
The Baba is a flirt indeed!

Within the walls my husband,
No jealousy when he's away,
This is what Nyonyas say,
One bullock cart two cows!

Pantun for Manek Mischiefs
by Baba Chan Eng Thai,
14 February 2017

Beaded collar for a bridal attendant

Image courtesy Ken Yap. First published in Phoenix Rising:
Narratives in Nyonya Beadwork from the Straits Settlements
*by Cheah Hwei-Fe'n. Singapore: NUS Press, 2010.
Photography by Sok Lin from Studio DL.*

The Bride Who Refused to Strip

Ten long days and nights have dragged by and the truth of the matter is that my marriage with Choon Neo has still not been consummated. Despite all the pomp and pageantry, the lavish rituals and incredible expense of a grand baba wedding, what am I meant to do if my bride refuses to even disrobe in front of me?

I am an inexperienced young man. The female sex is like the porcelain ware my mother amasses – fragile, colourful, decorative, but a mystery as to what all the fuss is about. It is the 1920s, well into the twentieth century – yet it's still the same old-fashioned nosiness, the same obsession with the bride's virginity. I have just two nights left to consummate the marriage. Otherwise there will be a lot of explaining to do, either on her part or mine. I don't know which is worse or more embarrassing – either she is not as innocent as she makes out to be or that I, Tony Tan Teik Seng, strong, virile, once the most eligible bachelor about town is hopelessly unable to... er... bed my wife.

My bride is pure and chaste – I'm absolutely sure. She has never had sex before with any man. She is just – very, very shy. So shy that till now, she won't even take off her top for me, never mind her underpants. Every night, when we go to bed, she sleeps at the very edge. Whenever I reach out to touch her, she flinches and squeals her disgust, pulling her blanket embroidered in a blaze of butterflies tighter around her neck.

"What's the matter? I won't hurt you, I promise. You... you must help me because I'm... er... new to this too," I try gentle persuasion.

She turns around and glares at me, her eyes flash disgust, she reverts to the same frigid position, staring at the pink curtains draped around her side of the bed.

If I attempt to go further, those beguiling eyes would moisten, then like an unexpected tropical storm, burst in a torrent of tears.

"Oh no... don't cry, please, please."

The sound and fury of sobs and blubbering continue.

"Please don't cry. I'll wait for you till you're less frightened, less shy, okay?"

I insist, "You've got to overcome your shyness. We can't go on like this."

She nods, weeping uncontrollably, her lower lip quivers and her body trembles. Her tears roll down and splash onto her pillow. I stare fascinated at the damp patch they create on her pillow – an expanding map of a soggy, fat Malaya. I yearn to touch those tearstained cheeks, feel her glowing skin.

"No rush, no hurry," I try to assure her.

She sobs quietly, her hair, worn in a bejewelled bun earlier, cascades around her face, a tantalising come-hither veil.

"We have our whole life ahead of us," I try to sound

the most patient red-blooded man on the planet.

That doesn't work. She starts bawling, her shoulders shuddering convulsively. She gasps for air as if she cannot breathe.

"Ssshhh... please stop crying. Hush..." I try to soothe her, panic rising in me as I have no idea how to deal with crying females.

I switch off the bedside lamp.

"Go to sleep. I won't disturb you anymore, I promise."

I perch close to the other side of the bed, staring into space. Frustrated, I swipe at the tasseled dingle-dangles which festoon the wedding bed, embroidered with auspicious symbols of pomegranates and flowers.

The wedding bed is magnificent but not very comfortable, painted in fiery red, lavishly decorated with tapestries and beaded baubles. The standing lamp throws a faint pinkish glow about the spacious room. It's obvious nothing has been spared to beautify the bridal boudoir. French lace curtains lovingly drape the windows, carpets swathe the wooden floor, and glass epergnes from England adorn the marble-topped tables, inlaid with shimmering mother-of-pearl. Two imposing cupboards with intricate wood carvings are backed up against the wall. In a far corner, a red washstand with gold carvings stands in solemn grandeur, holding a salmon-pink porcelain basin with peonies and more pomegranate patterns. Dainty monogrammed hand towels hang on its two handles.

A pair of graceful cranes in delicate stitches of white and gold wink at me as I lay my head on the pillow. Even the bolsters are decorated with intricate silver end pieces. The bridal room seems to pulsate with hope and fecundity. It is hard but I try my best to go to sleep.

All is still and quiet in the grand mansion. The hum of activity, occasional outbursts of laughter, the soft, lifting strains of *keroncong* have all died down. The last of the wedding guests, the long-winded ones who drink and talk forever, must surely have left by now. I toss about in my narrow half of the bed, restless, rejected and so alone. I can smell her enticing baby powder scent, feel her presence – my young bride sleeps just an arm's reach away. A soft moan and stifled sobs come from her side of the bed.

"Bah," I mumble under my breadth, take another swipe at the irritating dangling decorations, twinkling at me in the darkened room.

It has been the same every night since the wedding night. She rejects all my advances, cringes at the thought of me touching her. In the daytime, she is obedient and respectful to the elders and her in-laws, attentive to me, but at night, when we retreat to our bedroom, she becomes this ice-cold maiden, frigid and uninviting.

This is getting serious, a matter of some concern. If she weren't interested in marriage, why did she agree to it in the first place? Is it me? Am I moving too fast or too slow? Doing it all wrong? I wonder how men manage on their wedding nights with women they don't have a clue about. I certainly don't.

A year ago, I was a blissful bachelor with not a care in the world. I wasn't in a hurry to get married at all. I sensed something was going on when Mother became more preoccupied, and began to consult almanacs and fortune tellers. She made more trips to the temple to pray for extra blessings, she said. A few times, I caught her in hushed, secretive conversations with my aunts only to change the topic to something trivial when I stepped into the room.

Several times I bumped into Bibik Megawatt, the ebullient matchmaker who dropped by more frequently. In a raucous voice, with a dazzling smile that revealed two gold teeth, she boomed, "Hellooo... Ah Boy!"

She chuckled heartily, her eyes twinkling in excitement, the layers of flesh under her tight olive kebaya shaking in happy unison. Bibik Megawatt spoke only Baba Malay but she had learnt two sentences in English which she boomed at every potential bridegroom.

"Ambooi, you sooo big oredi!" she yelled flirtatiously, hands flapping, eyelashes batting.

And the next line, "Aiyooo, you sooo handsum boy oredi!" she screeched for the whole world to hear, glancing approvingly at me up and down. After flashing another electric smile, she waddled away into the house looking for my mother. I didn't give it much thought, just assumed Mother must be up to her usual tricks trying to marry off one of her myriad nieces or maybe even my sisters.

One morning, over breakfast, just as I was about to slurp up the remains of two softboiled eggs laced with divine Sarawak pepper, Mother announced she had found the perfect wife for me. I spluttered and coughed, almost choked on the eggs. Father noisily downed his cup of thick *kopi-oh*, beaming with anticipation, in total agreement with my mother. Once Father agreed with Mother, I knew it would be a tough battle for me.

"But... but Ma, why me ? I never said I'm looking for a wife! I thought you were busy trying to find husbands for Daisy and Ta Chi."

My two sisters needed far more assistance in this matrimonial business. Daisy, my younger sister was as vapid as they come, eternally preening in front of the mirror, shallow thoughts darting in and out of her pretty head, never staying long enough to form an opinion. Ta Chi, or Big Sister, on the other hand, was strong-willed and gutsy, attractive in a handsome sort of way. Not a problem with me that Ta Chi, or Dorothy as she is called, liked to dress in pants and man-sized shirts whenever she could, which really irked my parents. Father had even caught her once trying out his expensive cigars in the library, her legs propped up on his posh mahogany table in a most unbecoming manner.

"The stars are smiling in your favour, my dear son. She is a rooster and you a dragon," my mother continued, "a good match, the matchmaker assured us! It's not easy to find a bride for boys born in the Year of the Dragon, you know... "

"Not only that, the dates and time of your births are in perfect harmony. Not like that *si-dengil anak gua mia adik*, your stubborn cousin Leng Neo. Insisted on marrying Terence, the boy next door, even though their birth dates clash. And now, see *lah*, barren how many years! *Kek sim betul-betul...* Heartache only."

I didn't commit, just continued gulping down my meal then rushed off to the Club for rehearsals with the theatre and *dondang saying* troupe I was involved in.

Another time Mother changed tactics. She tried to persuade me by going on and on about the wealth and prestige of the bride's family, how we would become the richest family in all of Singapore and Malacca with the joining of our two families. Again that didn't work. I really didn't care much about conversations regarding money probably because my family already had so much of it.

I paid a little more attention when a delegation comprising Mother, two elderly aunts and Bibik Megawatt went to call on the potential bride's family and check out the young lady in question.

Mother came home with a glowing report, enraptured, singing praises of the young nyonya, Choon Neo.

"She is pure as a mountain spring. She is respectful,

well-mannered, absolutely beyond reproach. I watched her closely when she came out to serve us tea, the way she walked, the way she sat... *amboi, lembut-nya...* so ladylike.

"She's gentle and softspoken, not like those brazen tomboy types. Her voice is soft and melodious. She addressed us properly, used all the correct names. Very well brought up."

"What about her looks? She must be ugly if that's all you can say about her," I asked, mildly curious.

"Wait *lah*... I was coming to that. She is very *cantik*, a beautiful girl! Her face is oval-shaped like a melon seed, she has pearly white teeth, a most enchanting smile. And such dainty ankles and wrists.

"She is younger than you by a few years, educated to Standard Five. Then... *nasib baik*... her parents pulled her out of school to concentrate on becoming a good wife. She can cook, sew, *jaga rumah*... intelligent but not too educated, thank goodness! She is healthy and will bear many children," gushed my mother.

"A perfect match, my son," she ended triumphantly.

I was twenty-five years old, never kissed nor been kissed before. Perhaps my raging hormones were in overdrive that day. Being a filial son, and worn out by Mother's stubborn persistence and Father's gruff hints of longing for "the pitter-patter of grandchildren's feet", I found myself answering, "Okay, okay I agree. Please go ahead with the wedding plans, Ma."

A flurry of incessant activity took place in both households once the wedding date was fixed. Wedding invitation cards and *hantar sireh* were sent out personally and both the groom and bride's houses had to undergo spring cleaning, painting and redecorating. The all-important *chye kee*, a red bunting made of cotton with two artistically-tied lotuses on each side was hung over the main front door. Father ordered the servants to hoist up the family lanterns bearing our surname and the *tien teng*, the main lantern, to honour the King in Heaven in the main porch. Floors were scrubbed and brass handles, mirrors and furniture polished till they gleamed like newly-minted coins.

Mother ordered new sets of sarong kebayas for herself and her daughters for the wedding which dragged over twelve days. Daisy was in seventh heaven – what could be more important in life than a brand new wardrobe and the chance of attracting a potential suitor? Elder sister Ta Chi sulked and groaned, disliking any fuss and dressing up and fearful of the deluge of relatives. Vendors brought splendid batik sarongs in flamboyant colours and extravagant designs to the house for viewing. Kebaya artisans all over the Straits were sought after and commissioned with more orders, and frenzied trips were made to the jewelers for new *kerosangs*, pendants, earrings, bracelets and jewellery gifts.

The making of the kebayas required minute attention to detail which threw Mother and Daisy in a tizzy. If the material was mauve, what colours should the threads be for the embroidery motifs? A wrong colour combination would render the entire ensemble into a gaudy disaster. What about motifs of chrysanthemums in clusters with *kerawang*, or roses in an English summer garden setting – would that go better with peach instead of mauve? Or maybe old rose, a more romantic colour? If the motifs were a pair of embroidered dragons, would that be too '*ong*', too grand and fiery for the occasion? The womenfolk got more excited by the day and hour, the burden of preparations firmly on their shoulders. The patriarchs of both households dished out the money quietly for the wedding expenses, relieved to be spared much of the painstaking organisational details.

It was the preparation for the wedding feasts that demanded the most work. Four days before the wedding, the house was thrown open for the Hari Kupas Bawang, the Day of Peeling Onions. Onions, garlic, shallots, vital ingredients for the many sambals, curries, *sek bak* and *pongteh* dishes, lay in huge piles on the kitchen table waiting to be peeled. On Hari Menyambal, the Day of Preparing the Sambal, eighteen types of sambals were lovingly prepared over hot stoves amidst much noise and bantering. The large, breezy kitchen reverberated with the rhythmic pounding of spices and sambal blachan, grinding of fresh chili, slicing, chopping, toasting, washing, and joyful camaraderie. Relatives, cousins and close friends willingly attended to the countless chores, chatting noisily, laughing, teasing, scolding, flirting, catching up on the latest gossip.

I didn't really have to do anything except to participate in the very solemn Chiu Tau ceremony on the eve of the wedding. After the pre-nuptial dinner had ended at my home and all the guests had left, I performed the sacred Chiu Tau ceremony at midnight, dressed totally in white, paying homage to the gods, my ancestors and my parents.

Finally, the day everyone was waiting for arrived. Early in the morning, candles were lit to honour the almighty God, and after countless rituals, it was time to go and meet the bride. My bridegroom party made our way slowly to the bride's house in a resplendent procession – colourful banners streaming in the sunshine, gongs clashing loudly, lanterns bobbing above the crowd, huge silk umbrellas held high with mine in royal yellow. I was dressed like a Mandarin scholar with a star-shaped brooch pinned on my cap. All the gentlemen including the *Pak Chindek*, the master of ceremonies, wore elegant jackets, long gowns and mandarin hats, while the workers wore colourful batik tops and sarongs. A band of musicians made up the rear end of the procession, followed by relatives and close friends.

Crowds rushed out to stare at the procession weaving its way along the narrow streets. I felt like royalty, the king for the day sauntering gallantly down the road under my imposing yellow umbrella. On arrival at the bride's house, we were showered with yellow rice, sprinkled with scented water and invited into the house. I sat on a high-backed red chair, sipping tea and *leng chee kang*, a sweet drink to augur harmony and happiness, relieved the wedding had finally commenced and eager to meet my wife.

The air hung heavy with incense and smoke from the candles and joss sticks and thick with anticipation. The moment for the bride and groom to meet had finally arrived. The master of ceremonies flicks his fan open with a dose of drama and announced solemnly, "*Kia Sai, Sin Neo, lai chim pang,*" inviting the groom and bride to enter the bridal bedchamber. The *serunee* band struck up a poignant and solemn melody. I saw women crying, dabbing their eyes, yanking hankies out of their handbags or tucked within their kebayas. The tune was achingly sad. I felt an overwhelming sense of excitement at the thought of meeting her for the first time in my life.

The throngs of guests quickly made way for me as I rose to my feet to meet my bride. Through the parting crowd, I saw a slender young maiden, dressed in a magnificent outfit, moving gracefully towards me, swaying from side to side. She reached the centre of the room and paused. She was clad in a heavily embroidered gown in red, gold and burgundy. Her hair was upswept into a chignon decorated with a glittering crown of jewels and hairpins in gold and silver, topped with diamonds. Her bosom was covered with what must be the entire family heirloom – diamond-encrusted necklaces, thick strands of gold and precious stones, diamond and *intan kerosang* brooches and filigree gold pendants. Her hands were folded together under the long sleeves of her gown. I could not see her face as it was covered with a black lace veil. In time to the melancholic *serunee*, she slowly raised her arms and lowered her body in a graceful gesture of greeting, I lifted my clasped hands in response and followed her, mesmerised as she glided, swaying in a tantalising *lenggang lenggok* manner to our wedding boudoir.

The moment of truth arrived. We stood in the middle of the room facing each other. Gently, I reached out and lifted the veil. I stepped back, stunned. She was absolutely exquisite. A delicate sensitive face, sensuous red lips, cheekbones like an ethereal Javanese temple dancer. I could not see her eyes; they were downcast, as dictated by custom. I placed my hand under her chin and raised it a little. She lifted up long-lashed lids to meet my gaze. Her eyes were huge, teary captivating pools under arched eyebrows. I could have gazed at her forever... what is it they call when you go weak at the knees and your heart melts like butter in the sun and soars with the stars? Ahhh yes, love at first sight... I found what that was like at that encounter.

That moment now seems quite some time ago. I'm nervous, fighting against time here. It is the tenth night already. It's getting late and she's not even in the room. "Headache", she said, needed a drink of hot water and fresh air, and she hasn't returned. She's probably hoping I'd fall sound asleep by the time she comes back.

I need to do something soon. I was told that on the twelfth day of the wedding, both our mothers and senior ladies from both families will meet to examine the white cotton sheet from the wedding bed, to seek evidence the marriage was consummated. The mother-in-law of the bride will look for blood stains – proof of the bride's virginity. All done very discreetly and tactfully, as the womenfolk help themselves to the sireh leaves served on a tray complete with lime, gambier and sliced betel nuts. The lime comes in handy to test if the blood is real or false. If my mother is happy, she will arrange for a feast of *nasi lemak*, a delicious dish of steamed rice in coconut milk, to be sent to the bride's home, the sign that all is well, the bride is virtuous, untouched, and the honour of the family intact. However, from the way things are going for me, this theory is impossible to put to the test. As yet.

"*Neo, mana lu?* Where are you?" I called out.

No reply. Softly I pad out on naked feet to look. I don't see her anywhere, not at the balcony nor the window where one can enjoy the night breezes wafting in. I walk gingerly down the dark unlit corridor. At the end of the passage, I notice a door slightly ajar with a light inside. Stealthily, quiet as a ghost, I tiptoe towards that room, unsure whose room it is. I stop just outside and peep through the open door.

I freeze in horror at what I see. Am I having fantasies or hallucinating? For there lying on a simple spartan bed is my bride, semi-naked, her round breasts gleaming in the moonlight, a sarong half tossed invitingly above her long shapely legs. She looks fetching, like a young sultry temptress. I would have gone wild and been hers forever had she behaved like this to me. Who is she in bed with? Perhaps it's just the mirror she's looking at? Perhaps she's so shy she can only disrobe in front of the mirror, I rationalise.

In mounting horror, I see a hand reaching out for Choon Neo's slim waist. It rests tentatively there. But my bride doesn't squeal or cringe. Instead her eyes shine with an unseen tenderness, her lips curl enticingly upwards as she gazes lovingly at the... the thing, the object... beside her.

I take one step back. No harm done, just need to retrace my steps, no need to know, no more details needed. Tomorrow I'll get out of this, tell my parents, get my marriage nullified. Just move back and get away, I tell myself, my legs.

The curiosity is killing me. My body refuses to budge, my legs can't move. That hand around Choon Neo's waist looks smooth, hairless, almost familiar. Trembling, I push the door ajar very gently by one more inch. Just an inch more and I find out that the hand belongs to my sister, Ta Chi. Equally naked, her right leg reaches out to coil around my bride's body in a slithery embrace.

Macam udang kena air panas
(Like shrimps being boiled)
Meaning: Girls getting excited

Nangis air mata darah pun tak guna lagi
(Crying blood tears now is hopeless)
Meaning: Once the deed is done,
even if you shed tears of blood, it is useless.

Wedding bed for the bridal bedchamber

Butterfly wedding bed hangings

Cushion covers

Beaded tray cover

All images above courtesy the Peranakan Museum, Singapore

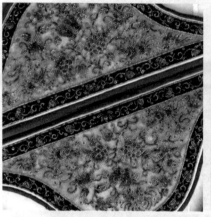

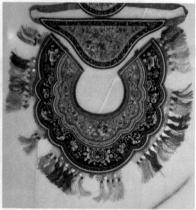

A pair of metallic beaded wedding knee pads

Embroidered collar of wedding attire for a pageboy or pagegirl

Bridal bed tie hangings

The Stump in the Hole under the Casuarina Tree in the Garden of the Mansion by the Sea

The sea breeze is the first thing that assails your senses when you walk into Sherwood Villa. Its coolness lifts your spirits, its playfulness brings a smile to your lips as it dishevels your hair. The familiar salty tang of sea spray and the mewing cries of the seagulls sing to me I have come home.

Sherwood Villa. My family home and the most precious place in the world to me. I was born here in this palatial mansion by the sea, in the master bedroom upstairs with the view of the garden blazing with bougainvillea and hibiscus. My grandfather, Lim Beng Yam, bought this bungalow in 1912 from a movie tycoon from Hong Kong. The eldest son of a rich family, my grandpa, through hard work, grit and perseverance, built an even bigger empire in rubber, tin mining, trade and plantations. He had that Midas touch, succeeding in many business ventures. He became a renowned philanthropist, donating large sums to schools, hospitals, infrastructure and the underprivileged. He invested in property and owned several houses in Malacca and Singapore but it was this magnificent estate he loved the most.

"Ouch," I stumbled over a crack in the driveway leading up to the grand country home.

"Never happened before... humph, cracks everywhere," I grumbled as I picked myself up with a bruised left knee.

I limped up to the entrance, placed my getaway duffel bag on the marble bench and pressed the doorbell. Several times. No one appeared.

"Hellooo, Ko Ko," I yelled, calling for my elder brother.

Strange. Usually Ah Yeng, our amah, would come running out to the front, wiping her hands on her *samfoo* top, beaming with joy.

"*Wah, Ah Nui, nei farn lei lah!*" she'd bellow, grinning from ear to ear, her kindly eyes disappearing into her cheeks, baggy, black pants flapping crazily as the sea breeze caught playfully onto her.

She called me *Ah Nui* which means 'daughter' in Cantonese, even though she was unmarried and sworn to a life of celibacy. She had served my family for as long as I could remember, already employed here before I was born. She was always the first person to welcome me whenever I could escape from my job in the tough advertising industry in Singapore.

"*Ah Yeng, Ah Yeng-ah? Ko Ko...* anybody home?" I called again.

I sat on the cool marble and waited. The verandah was

spacious with columns, three arches and a trough, which I remember, overflowed with marigolds and lantanas. There used to be a rattan table and wicker chairs. Grandma occasionally entertained her friends to scones, sandwiches and afternoon tea at this elegant space. Every evening, Grandpa had his 'sundowners' here – two *stengahs* of the best Johnny Walker Black Label whisky and soda water although the *stengah* or so-called 'halves' tended to veer towards whisky most of the time.

It was on this very bench, I reminisced, more than twenty years ago, Grandpa told me why he had named his mansion, Sherwood Villa.

"My father was a very pragmatic man. He decided straightaway that as we were a British colony the way to succeed was to learn the way of the British. When I was sixteen, he put me on the steamer, this mighty ship run by the P and O and sent me to England to study. I was petrified. I was brought up an ordinary baba boy and had never ever met an 'ang mo' before. This ship was full of foreign devils, all going home to Mother England, and I was the only Asian on board! At dinner time, the men dressed in formal dinner jackets and the women wore evening gowns and sparkled with jewellery. Can you imagine my terror when I sat down to dinner the first time and there were all these instruments laid out in two rows to my right and left... a whole array of knives, forks and spoons! What was I to do? All my life, I ate with my fingers at home! Luckily Pa had lectured me, 'When in Rome, do as the Romans do', so I watched closely and copied everything they did.

But the worst was yet to come. For the main course, the waiter placed a spring chicken on my plate! I mean a whole chicken, imagine that! My mother always served chicken in bite-sized pieces whether it was chicken curry or ayam pong teh or ayam buah keluak. I'd never seen an entire chook before, bluish pupils eyeing me through half-closed lids, its legs trussed up against its bump. I watched the lady to my right and to my left and proceeded to carve my chicken. The bloody chicken sprung out of my plate! It waltzed giddily around on the floor and stopped near a greenish gown. I wanted to crawl under the table in shame.

But here is where I take off my hat to the English. In typical stiff upper lip fashion, they pretended not to notice. The woman seated on my right... must be a duchess what with her tiara and white gloves, dripping with diamonds, commented, 'Lovely evening, isn't it?'

I went down on my knees, searched for my chicken, picked it up and put it back on my plate. I managed to cut a sliver of thigh and chewed sheepishly on it. No one said anything nor raised an eyebrow, they all continued to make polite conversation. Only the distinguished, old gentleman sitting opposite remarked as he gave me a wink, 'Jolly good, ol' chap! It does say spring chicken on the menu,' before he downed his glass of champagne.

From that moment on, I knew I'd be alright. Wherever I was going, if these people had this kind of sense of humour, I would survive. And I did. That's why I love a lot of things

English... can't think of a nicer name for this house than the forest where Robin Hood lived. I wanted to call it Camelot but your grandma said that was too much, we are not royalty."

I chuckled as I pictured Grandpa crawling on his knees under the table on a mighty ocean liner, gingerly lifting one slinky gown after another looking for his dinner. I glanced around the verandah. It had an air of weariness now, the table legs chewed up, the wicker chairs frayed around the edges. Dead leaves cluttered the long curving driveway. The flower trough was completely smothered in weeds. This verandah was the last place I saw Grandpa, waving farewell in his white t-shirt and old sarong. His last words to me were, "Come home soon, *sayang*. This is your home, remember that. Sherwood Villa will always be here. Bye!"

When I learnt he had a deadly stroke, I rushed home on the first flight I could get out of Singapore but I was too late, he had passed away. I was too late to say goodbye.

The grating noise of bolts and padlocks and then the huge teak door opened. My brother, Seong, stood there, red-eyed, unshaven, the beginnings of a paunch round his once trim waist.

"Hi Sis, I guessed it was you. Why didn't you call first?" he grumbled in a hoarse voice.

"I did. Several times but no reply. Did you just wake

up? It's almost noon... what a cushy life you lead, Ko Ko!" I teased him, always happy to see Seong again.

"Where's Ah Yeng?" I asked as I stepped into the cavernous main hall, imposing with its formal portraits of family members and silk scrolls from China on the walls. A bevel-edged marble top table stood in the centre, ringed by six stools and alongside the walls, blackwood benches studded with mother of pearl inlay.

"Ah Yeng? Oh, she's left. It's a long story. C'mon in, you can have the main guest room. I'm going back to sleep, I had a late night."

I wanted an explanation on Ah Yeng's absence. Before I could say a word, he grumbled, "I made a lot of money last night, Sis. At the final round, I threw in everything, can't go wrong, I was having such fantastic luck! *Celaka*, guess what? I lost it all. Everything. Bloody hell!"

He stomped sulkily up the majestic winding staircase designed by Grandpa, inspired by grand heritage houses in England, and slammed the bedroom door shut.

I sank down on a marble stool in despair. Great wealth lasts for only three generations, the Chinese say. My brother Lim Gan Seong looked like he certainly was the last. He had inherited this magnificent property which Grandpa and Pa had looked after so lovingly. In its entirety. My two sisters and I did not get even a slimmest share. Seong lived alone like the lord of a country estate after our parents passed away, with a staff of servants, cooks and driver. The staff size diminished every time I returned. I was in the unfortunate position of watching the favoured son squander the family inheritance away.

From a young age, Seong, a cute precocious child, was spoilt by his mother, both grandmothers and everyone around. My parents desperately wanted a boy; after two daughters, the arrival of a son brought much joy and celebration. Seong was treated like a little emperor, whatever he desire, his wish was granted. While daughters were expected to do household chores, Seong, the only son, was exempted from having to lift a finger. No matter what he did, he was never wrong nor punished.

The pampering and over-indulgence took its toll. He grew up, self-centred and arrogant, used to getting his way all the time. Endowed with an immense fortune, he lived a dissipated lifestyle, philandering, squandering money, night-clubbing, changing girlfriends like underwear and gambling.

Anxious old aunts in hush-hushed phone calls tried to persuade me to talk to him.

Get him married quickly.

Make him settle down.

Dia mia perempuan suma gold diggers... his girlfriends only see dollar sign... whole of Malacca gossiping! Sampeh Singapore. Malu sia! Shameful.

Apa ni Si-Seong kejair kejair perempuan all over town? Ta malu-eh?! Chasing everything in skirts, no shame-ah?

I was born a year after Seong. It was hard for me to scold or lecture my older brother. Besides, I loved and adored my brother – we were very close, playmates in our growing-up years. But at every visit home recently, I stumbled upon worrying signs.

When I returned last year for Cheng Beng, an annual ritual held in remembrance of our ancestors, I was astonished to see two dazzling new cars – a Mercedes and a Jaguar parked along the driveway. I knew Seong, crazy about cars and a speed freak, already owned a BMW coupe. With his newfound wealth, I suppose he wanted to indulge further but this was excessive.

Another time, I came home to Sherwood Villa for the death anniversary of my father. Seong was out that evening at his usual jaunts, the cabarets and clubs at Sultanah Road. I was upstairs on the balcony enjoying the view of the shimmering sea on a moonlit night and the sound of the rustling trees. I felt an intense loneliness, recalling the days when the mansion was filled with people, laughter and music, the clack-clack of mahjong tiles, but now only this lonesome silence except for the waves and the wind.

I decided to go for a walk on the beach – it was beautiful in the moonlight. Walking across the extensive grounds, I heard an unfamiliar sound – giggly laughter interspersed with shrieks. Two figures emerged, weaving in and out of the coconut palms near the sea wall. It looked like a scene from a Bollywood movie except they were half-naked, my brother staggering about half-drunk, chasing a slip of a girl screaming in mock terror. I turned abruptly back to my room.

More indiscretions awaited. On a recent visit, in the formal dining room, once the focus of magnificent *tok panjang* banquets, I chanced upon a skimpy red cloth on the dining table. I thought the maids had forgotten to put the cloth away after polishing the silver. Then, I realised it was womens' panties and threw it in the trash bin in disgust.

Worse, a pair of silk stockings was draped carelessly over the altar table in the ancestral hall. These women Seong brought home had no respect for the family! This was the *thia abu*, the most sacred part of the house, where we honoured our ancestors in daily rituals and elaborate ceremonies. Here we knelt with joss sticks and made food offerings on important occasions. A portrait of my grandfather, the patriarch of the Lim clan, dressed in a dapper western suit and tie, hung above the altar table. Portraits of Grandma in *baju panjang*, my parents and other deceased family members lined the walls in a montage. What would our ancestors think of us?

When I confronted Seong over this, his reply was, "Oh shut up, little sister. Thank your lucky stars it wasn't a condom."

My aunts were right, I had to intervene. I traced my finger along the serrated patterns of the Carrera marble table, imagining towering pinnacles and plunging waterfalls and felt resentful. Why me? Why is it always me of all people to rein him in? I am just a daughter, an outsider once I married into another family, while my brother Seong was the pride of the Lim clan, the male offspring tasked to perpetuate the family line.

Big brother's beauty sleep was taking a long time. I felt peckish. No more Ah Yeng and no servants with trays of coffee, *kueh* and snacks. As I headed for the kitchen through a covered walkway, I did a double take and strode back into the house – to the second hall. Something was missing. I could swear it wasn't an empty space before. There used to be something against that wall.

Where was the dresser? It was no longer there! The one with the ornate canopy, wood spires and mirrors. My favourite, as it was so over the top! It even had a coat of arms with a unicorn and a lion carved in wood. As a child, I imagined I was a princess whenever I gazed into the mirror, framed with cut-glass stars. Grandma preened and powdered here. She kept a jar of *bedak sejuk* in this dresser. She would grind the tiny granules of rice powder into a paste with a bit of water and slather it on her face. Then, she would call us and dab the rest of it all over us amidst our protests. I used to loathe that *bedak sejuk* paste as it gripped my face in a tight mask making it impossible to smile. Grandma told me I would inherit her dresser one day.

There were more things missing. I remember the two beautiful *almeiras*, Dutch cupboards where my mother kept the linen, crystal and silverware. They were gone too. I was furious – how could he? How dare Seong give away the contents of our family home?

"Where's Grandma's dresser gone? The one with the *bedak sejuk*?" I screamed at Seong before he even got halfway down the staircase, rubbing his forehead, nursing a hangover.

"Whoa... *Garang betul*... why so fierce? What dresser?"

"Stop pretending. You know very well what I mean. The dresser in the second hall is gone. So are the antique cupboards!"

"Oh, those bulky things. I'm sick of them! *Benci sekali.*"

"You could have at least asked us first! You have three sisters, remember? It's not for you to simply give our things away."

"Eh listen, Eldest Sister and Second Sister have emigrated to God-knows-where and you, little sister, live in a tiny flat in tiny Singapore. What the hell do you want the stuff for?"

"They're not stuff! They belong to the family. Stop swearing."

"There's tons more. Every damn thing here is antique, including you, Sis, if you don't get a man soon. What a freaking grump!"

"When you inherited this place, I didn't hear you complain!"

"You're jealous you didn't get this place, aren't you? I

got it all. Hahaha."

"How dare you discard our family possessions! As if they don't mean a thing."

"They don't. And I didn't give them away. I sold them."

"This is our family home, our *rumah abu*, you were entrusted to look after it."

"Do the ancestors care? They're all dead. Kaput. Those urns for the ashes will fetch a lot of money."

"Don't you dare sell those, you moron!" I blasted him.

"Stop nagging or you can leave right now!"

I grabbed my bag and stormed out of the house, spitting my words at him, "Well goodbye then!"

I could hear my brother shouting at the entrance, trying to use his charm to entice me to stay over.

"Hey, Sis come back. Come back *lah*. I was just joking. How are you going back to Singapore?"

I did not talk to Seong for several months after that incident. One evening, exhausted from a tough day at the office, I was foraging for leftovers in my fridge when I got a phone call from Seong.

"Hello, Sis. Can you come up to Malacca this weekend? It's the grand opening of my brand new restaurant."

This news startled me. Finally, he was doing something! Actually working for a change.

"That's great news. What kind of restaurant?"

"Nyonya. My business partner and I are going to open a nyonya restaurant. Big crowd puller you know, nyonya cuisine!"

"Nyonya food? That's difficult commercially and too labour intensive."

"Easy *lah*. Just make the same old dishes but name everything 'nyonya'. Nyonya assam fish, nyonya fried prawns, nyonya chicken. *Taroh saja lah*. If you say it is 'nyonya', then it is."

"It won't work."

"These dumb tourists won't know."

"People aren't that stupid. Who are your chefs?"

"I'm bringing in some cheap foreign workers."

"Oh my goodness."

"Can *lah*. Just look at some recipe books."

"It's not as simple as that."

"Ahh, it will be okay. Have I ever failed?"

"I wouldn't know. You've never been put to the test."

"Anyway, nite nite. Got to go – I've a hot date with sexy Fei Fei. She's gorgeous. You really should get a boyfriend, Sis, you're such a grouch. See you this weekend."

"I can't make it, it's too short notice. Please be careful, Ko."

"Of what?"

"I don't know. Just don't rush into things."

"Don't worry *lah*, I'm born lucky. Bye bye."

I could not attend the grand opening of the Baba Seong Restaurant as I had deadlines to meet. If only he knew how much I wanted him to succeed. He needed a job, a project, anything to keep him away from the gambling den. The news I received from friends in Malacca was unnerving. He had rented a huge space at an exorbitant rate and spent a fortune hiring interior decorators. The foreign cooks didn't have a clue about nyonya food and came up with bizarre culinary pretensions. The locals avoided the restaurant and the tourists could smell a rat – the dishes all looked and tasted the same, laden with chili and onions.

One afternoon, as I was rushing to a business lunch, I got a call from Chim Po, my grandaunt from Ujong Pasir, Malacca. In her mid-eighties, still sharp and feisty, she ranted agitatedly, "*Aiyee cerkik darah! Lu mia celaka Si-Seong, dah masuk angin! Gila. Brani ambik gambair di tok abu..*"

"Chim Po, what's happened?"

More ranting and background noise, then she thrust the phone to her daughter, Diana.

"Hi Aunty Diana. What has Seong done this time?"

"That *gila* brother of yours! He has taken Grandpa's portrait from our *Thia abu* and hung it up in his stupid restaurant! Has he gone nuts?" Diana shrieked at me.

In a voice cold as ice, I talked to Seong that night on the phone.

"Seong, I want you to succeed, believe me. But please, please put Grandpa's portrait back where it belongs."

"Whaa-at? Why can't I use it in my restaurant? It looks nice. Very distinguished looking."

"Grandpa is not a piece of décor. You've taken his portrait from the ancestral home and that's unforgiveable."

"You've got this sentimental thing about the dead, you know. It's just collecting dust. I own Sherwood Villa, remember?"

"The things in it are not yours – it's not stated in the will. But I don't really care anymore. They are just objects – you can have them. But show some respect to the memory of Grandpa. Is nothing sacred to you?"

"Want an honest answer?" he asked.

I slammed down the phone on him.

A year passed by. The pace of working life was relentless, a demanding schedule of endless deadlines. I felt trapped on a carousel, unable to get off but the work helped take my mind away from home.

I did not return to Sherwood Villa for Chinese New Year nor All Souls' Day. It was too painful for me to see the decay, the loss of a way of life I had known and my brother's behaviour and financial ruin.

One morning I received an urgent text message from Seong:

Sis, something terrible has happened. Come home ASAP.

As the taxi drove through the massive wrought iron gate and up the familiar driveway once more, I was relieved to see Sherwood Villa still standing. She looked like a tired old dame, her cobwebbed walls covered in mould, her paintwork peeling. Bat and bird droppings littered the floor. Grandpa's wicker chairs had been replaced by plastic stools.

"Anybody home?" I called.

The front door was ajar. I stepped into the sullen silence.

"Is everything alright, Seong? Where are you?" I shouted. I walked through the gloomy, musty halls searching for my brother.

At the Great Hall, I paused. It still looked charming, sunshine filtering in through the bay windows. Strains of my parents' favourite waltzes drifted into my mind – they used to throw fabulous parties here, a live band playing while guests danced the cha cha, rumba, waltz and the joget. Grandpa had let me taste my first sip of champagne here.

"Over here, Sis. In the garden!" I heard Seong's voice.

I stepped out into the garden and was shocked at the war zone. The garden, vibrant with hibiscus, frangipani and orchids in its heyday, was now an eyesore, a morass of mud, gravel and a dying lawn. A hole, six feet deep, gaped in the centre. Scattered about were steel drums, tins of paint, tiles and plastic sheets. Grandpa's rose arbour was taken over by a cement mixer and a wire mesh frame. Beside them, a wheelbarrow stood with plastic bags of unfinished tea, straws sticking out, strung on its handle.

"What are you doing?" I exploded in dismay.

"Nothing. I'm just trying to cover back this hole," he mumbled, trying to sound nonchalant.

Seong limped up, dripping with sweat, eyes wild and panicky. He held a huge spade in his soft, feminine hands.

"What is happening here?" I demanded.

"Oh didn't you know, Sis? I'm going into the budget hotel business. Big money, budget hotels! Nyonya restaurant went bankrupt. Useless *bodoh* chefs!"

"Budget hotel? What's it got to do with this... this giant hole?"

"It's a swimming pool! Can't have a budget hotel without a swimming pool, you know."

"You're turning Sherwood Villa into... a what? A budget hotel?" I asked, incredulous.

"Why not? So many rooms here what. Sis, I need to borrow money. I have to hire workers to cover up the damn hole."

"What happened to the swimming pool idea?"

"This bloody hole is a nightmare. All my luck is draining into it. I've been cursed!"

"Cursed? What do you mean?"

"First, Fei Fei the bimbo fell inside the hole. Now she wants to sue me."

"Is she alright?"

"Small matter, her knee cap broke. Into three pieces. But only one knee what. The other one is fine."

"If you say so."

"Then... er... then recently one of the workers fell into the hole."

"Did he break his knees too?"

" Er no... he died. Broke his neck or something like that. It's become a police case. Absurd."

"This is serious. Investigating you for negligence, right? Not murder, I hope."

"I'm frightened, Sis. You've got to help me."

"Frightened of who? The police?"

"Nah, coffee money will fix that. I'm frightened for me.. it's going to be me next... I just know it.. it always happens in threes."

He rubbed his hands nervously over his face, fingernails caked with dirt. I had never seen him in this state before.

"Just cover up the hole. There'll be no more accidents," I suggested.

He blurted, "All the workers have run away. *Hantu, hantu,* screaming like idiots. The place's haunted. It's that thing they dug up. That grotesque thing. Someone has laid a curse on me!"

"What did they find?"

"An ugly black thing. A rotting stump."

"A stump?"

"Yeah. Someone planted it there. Black magic! Someone jealous of me!"

"Where did you find it?"

"Under the casuarina tree. One of the workers dug it out. Fool ran away screaming *pukau pukau*. Never came back. The rest bolted too."

"You've done it, you've blown it, now you've really angered Grandpa. Put it back, quick! Where is it?"

"What do you mean?"

"Where's the stump? I hope you've NOT thrown it away."

"It was inside that wheel barrow. I told the workers to get rid of it."

He started running towards the wheel barrow. I followed as fast as I could, gravel crunching under our feet. Inside lay a bundle of rotting calico wrapped around something. Seong picked it up.

"It's still here. Those blinking clowns, never follow orders! What is it? What to do with it? Destroy it? Get a *bomoh*?"

"It's Grandpa's foot, you idiot! You dug out Grandpa's foot!"

"Whaaaat?" he dropped it with a thud, face turning ashen.

"Arrghhh, pick it up! You dropped Grandpa's foot, you idiot! No respect!" I gasped.

Wincing, he picked the bundle up gingerly and held it at a distance, face screwed up in disgust.

"Now bury it. Back in the same place. Under the first casuarina tree," I ordered.

"When Grandpa died, didn't they bury him? Cremate him? What's his foot doing hanging around here?" asked

Seong, looking as if he was about to throw up.

"Grandpa had severe diabetes toward the end of his life and had his right foot amputated, didn't you know?"

"No one told me."

"That's because you never kept in touch gallivanting all over Europe. Six years supposedly getting a degree in law and you never bothered."

"I thought Grandpa died... er... intact."

"He was an amputee. I came home to visit him after the operation. He was upbeat, moving around on a wheelchair. He told the servants to bury his foot under the casuarina tree. He gave strict orders that no one was allowed to remove it."

"Arrrggghh, I am cursed. Grandpa has cursed me! I am ruined forever!"

"Stop blabbering. Hurry up, put back Grandpa's foot where it belongs," I ordered my terrified brother.

That day was one of the most brilliant days I had had in a long time. I had never seen Seong work so hard in his entire life, hacking desperately away at the hardened earth.

I visited Sherwood Villa again recently. Three years had passed since my last visit there and the kerfuffle over Grandpa's amputated foot. In that time, I had gone overseas, obtained a postgraduate degree and made a career switch. I wrote to Seong several times from abroad but he never bothered to reply. After three years in the UK, I wasn't quite sure what to expect when I returned to my homeland and drove to Malacca to visit Sherwood Villa, a three hours' drive away from Kuala Lumpur in the 1970s.

When I reached the destination, I was puzzled as I couldn't recognise the place. The skeletal frame of Sherwood Villa was there but that was all. The walls had collapsed and the roof had fallen in. The lawn was completely covered with fresh red earth. There was something else missing... what always greeted me when I arrived. The salty tang of the sea. I missed its smell and taste and its gentle, welcoming breezes. I walked around one side of the corpse-like mansion only to find that even the sea had gone! In its place a vast tract of flat, reclaimed land stretching as far as the eye could see. The sea which had given my family and the generations before such pleasure, twinkled a great distance away.

My eyes searched for the row of casuarinas. Was Grandpa's foot safe and undisturbed? He wouldn't be too happy if it was moved again. There was no sign of any casuarina trees, the garden was razed and flattened in anticipation of a huge construction project. A signboard confirmed it all as I walked out of Sherwood Villa for the last time. It said SOLD.

"This is your home, remember that. Sherwood Villa will always be here," Grandpa's words echoed hauntingly in my ears as I walked sadly away.

Nasik sua jadi buboh
(Rice has become porridge)
Meaning: It is too late to regret,
no use crying over spilled milk.

Bukit brapa tinggi pun cangkul cangkul nanti rata
(However high the hill, one can still hoe it down)
Meaning: No matter how much wealth
you have, you can lose everything.

A fully beaded Baba belt

Embroidered Baba slippers

A baba trouser sash

A magnifying glass cover

Two manek fob stopwatch covers. The stopwatch was used for timing racehorses.

All images above courtesy Ken Yap

Beaded valance

Two teapots, a chupu and a plate

A kamcheng, a container for holding food or water

Wealthy Baba families in the 19th and early 20th century liked to commission their crockery from China with colourful motifs that suited their tastes.
Left: A specially commissioned plate

All images above, except middle row, courtesy Ken Yap

The Merry Wives and Concubines of Patriarch Baba Gan

Wife Number One

Another wife? He wants to get another wife? *Siau eh ang...* *loh mor liau...* Fifty over years old, still don't know how to behave... shameful!

Twenty years of a good marriage and he tells me he wants to marry again. Of all people, to his favourite concubine! How do you think I feel? He told me, it's okay... this what's-her-name Loo Loo is a nice sweet girl. I'm sure she is very sweet to him – his business empire stretches all the way from Penang to Phuket, Medan in the west, Borneo to the east and as far south as Singapore and Batavia. He is worth millions of dollars. Who won't be sweet with all that money?

"She will respect you and acquiesce to you in all matters," he assured me, "You will always be the First, Wife Number One, the Matriarch of this house."

Think I'm stupid or what? I refused. Cried, howled, ranted but he was adamant. I threatened to kill myself. He didn't kick up a fuss over that. *Celakak!* How can he do this to me? I have been a flawless wife. A good, virtuous and responsible wife. I make sure this household with its cooks, servants, slave girls, butlers, stable hands, drivers and gardeners runs smoothly like clockwork. Every day, he is served the most splendid nyonya meals, coffee is exactly the way he likes it every morning, clothes are beautifully pressed, cars all polished gleaming in the sunshine, his race horses in top form. His country homes in Penang Hill and beach bungalows at Tanjong Bungah and Batu Ferringhi are ever ready, fresh flowers in the front hall.

I send out the *kuehs* and gifts when a family celebration comes around, I organise the parties, teas and grand dinners for his business associates and his high-class British friends. I make sure the ancestor worship rituals are scrupulously carried out. I pray to all the dead souls of this family. He's too busy with his business and extra-curricular activities he doesn't even know his children's birthdays! And this is my reward? A second wife? I absolutely oppose it. His own father had seven wives but this is the 1930s, it's about time this practice is stopped.

The stubborn fool... he keeps pestering me, probably because that... that... dare I say it.... say it *lah*, that bitch is pestering him. Now he has found another excuse – he wants a son. We have three daughters, no sons and of course, it is my fault. His Loo Loo is healthy and strong, she will give us many sons, he says. Her sons will acknowledge me as their mother. I've been eating *p'eng tor*, pig's stomach, hoping I'll get a boy. But what's the use when he is totally disinterested in our matrimonial bed?

Then along comes this brilliant idea... actually it wasn't my idea... it was Bibik Chichak's, my cousin from Batu Berendam who came to visit. I was moaning and groaning about my husband's ill intentions when she suggested, "*Toksa lu kek sim. Lu pegi cari satu bini lah kasi dia...*"

What a brilliant idea! Why didn't I think of it? Allow him a second wife, give him my blessings but it is I who will choose the wife for him.

My husband Baba Gan was taken aback at first. He agreed on condition she was young, beautiful and could bear him sons. When he left for the races that Sunday, I quickly called Ah Seng, our Hainanese cook, to write to his brother in China. Go to the remote villages, find a simple country girl and send her over as soon as possible. Tell him to find someone naïve, preferably in her teens without any ideas yet in her brain, a plain looking girl who won't grab too much attention. If he succeeds, I will reward him handsomely.

When the prospective bride arrived at the doorstep – of the back door, on my orders – I couldn't help smirking with delight. Ah Seng's brother really overdid it... such a dumpy thing, a country bumpkin in a shabby *samfoo*, doesn't even know how to hold a tea cup in her clumsy fingers. Her thick hair had been brushed and her face scrubbed clean but I could spot dirt in her fingernails. When I asked her where her things were, she said she was carrying all her possessions with her. In that tiny patchwork bag? How pathetic.

I treat her very well, have to make sure she's my ally. We

women must unite to face all life's obstacles. This peasant is docile and hardworking, grateful for being rescued out of some poverty-stricken dump.

Baba Gan was not pleased though when I presented his new bride to him. He barked, "What is this? I set three conditions and you haven't met them."

"Yes, I have. You said she must be young, beautiful and can bear sons. She is young and will bear you sons."

"And the second condition?" he queried, shooting a quick look at the pudgy candidate with her flat nose and gauche behaviour, staring agape at the wall tapestries of buxomy shepherdesses and sheep in bucolic country gardens with rolling meadows in the background.

I responded, "Beauty is in the eye of the beholder."

"Ummphh," he grunted, not a very good answer considering he's a lawyer. And that was it. Young firm body and already he gets horny... think I don't know... that's my husband for you.

Wife Number Two

I never hungry here in new home. Not like in China. In my village in China always no food. Day after day eat rice with water, a bit of soya sauce. Sometimes no rice when big famine come. Must look for rat, bug, tree bark. Many people die nothing to eat. Now stomach okay but big pain in my heart. I miss my father mother sister. What to do, I born a girl, is a porblum. Father mother want boy but get girl, girl all the time. When I born, mother want to kill me, use the cord that come along with baby stomach. Father stop mother. Bring me up till cannot anymore. Sell me off for three bags rice and cooking oil. Father say I will have better life cross the sea to Nanyang.

In this big house I no see no smell hunger. Everybody always eating. Always eating cooking eating all the time. Food always chili very hot not like Chinese food. Number One Wife very fierce order me do this do that, treat me like servant. "*Ngei*," mother always say. Endure, women must endure. Life is suffering, that why when baby born baby crying not laughing.

Wife Number One

Everything was peaceful again after I procured Wife Number Two for Baba Gan. She is strong as an ox and she learns fast. She can stir the gooey durian cake with the strength of three men. She has learnt how to pound the *rempah* spices to perfection. She knows how to slice the turnips, carrots and cabbage at lightning speed for my favourite *ju hu char*. It's her job now to supervise the kitchen staff, look after the children and the house when I play *cherki* with my friends. I have more time on my hands but I make sure I know everything that goes on, nobody farts without me knowing.

A year after she arrived, Number Two gave birth to a boy who looks just like Baba Gan. My husband was very pleased and rewarded me with a two carat diamond ring. The next year she got pregnant again and gave birth to another boy. This son looks like her *pulak*, tubby ugly thing with his mother's flat nose. The boys call me Mother and call her Aunty. That was the agreement.

Everything was fine in this grand mansion on Millionaire Avenue, Penang. My husband's family line was assured. His good luck and keen business sense have led to even greater fortunes in sugar, coffee, coconut oil, tin and rubber. His philanthropy has brought him prestigious awards such as Justice of the Peace bestowed by the English king. I was really pleased with the way things had turned out.

But the peace lasted only a short time. Baba Gan is restless again! Wah, two wives also not enough! He's keeping a few concubines, I know, but *gua boh chap*. What I don't see, I don't know. Now he says he wants to marry again!

One afternoon, can you believe it? Who comes sauntering into my house leaning on my husband's arm, looking bashful, simpering away as though it were her wedding day? Why that... that wretched concubine of his, that tenacious slut Loo Loo! In a red *kwa*, a Chinese bridal dress with gold embroidery, with diamonds in her hair, ears, fingers, throat! Baba Gan tells me no argument and no discussion – she is now his Wife Number Three! Despicable! Disgraceful.

Wife Number Two

Baba Gan good to me but now he complain I very fat always pregnant. Wah so clever to talk! I donch know how to answer him back. I very heart pain because my two son treat me like Aunty. I so suffer bring them into the world.

But this is my fate.

Big trouble in the house yesterday. Baba Gan bring into house another woman. Pretty but look like toy. Too much war paint on face. Number One Wife very angry like dragon breathing fire, come inside kitchen scold everybody. Baba Gan order Number One and me drink tea served by Painted Face. Oh oh... tea ceremony mean Painted Face now official Wife Number Three. I donch care how many wives he collect – very good – no need to disturb me. But Number One now become Black Face, make everybody scare only.

Wife Number One

These sugary, saccharine types are the deadliest. The sweeter their flattery, the deadlier their knives in your back. Baba Gan didn't even bother to ask my permission this time – just brought this leech home and ordered me to go through the tea ceremony. The Loo Loo woman pretended to be so respectful while serving tea, showering me with false flattery – "*Nei Nei*, your figure is very well-maintained, just like your house", "You still have so much hair – for your age," or "*Nei Nei*, you have a dignified look, you look like your husband's mother." All back-handed compliments, think I don't know!

I wanted to throw the tea into her smug face. I can see right through her but I must stay calm. She is just his latest plaything. As long as I am Number One Wife here, she cannot challenge my position.

This mansion has many rooms, corridors and courtyards. I don't have to see her face except at meal times.

I cannot stand her artificial ways, the way she walks and talks, flirting, playing with my husband... even under the table! I know because her foot crawled up my thigh under my sarong the other day. I screamed like crazy, I thought it was a snake. *Siau char boh*... cock-eyed or what? Can't even aim properly for my husband's foot.

I was beautiful too but many years have passed since then. Loo Loo has beauty and youth in her favour, her skin is creamy-smooth as tofu, she has a shapely hour glass figure. She speaks in a husky, breathless voice. And the way she moves, gyrating her hips, even the driver and male servants cannot concentrate on their work. My husband will die of a heart attack if he doesn't watch out.

All my life I scrimped over my husband's money, now she spends it like water. She openly defies and ignores me, has no respect for her seniors and does not follow the rules in this house. Whatever she wants, my besotted husband will buy for her, the most extravagant jewellery, cheongsams of pure silk and exquisite brocade from Shanghai, expensive Western clothes and ball gowns from London and Paris. She refuses to wear the sarong – hates all that cloth bundled around her legs, she says.

I've got to win him back or if not, at least break her hold over him. I must think of something. There's got to be a way.

Wife Number Three

Mother would be so proud of me if she were alive today. I did it! Hit the jackpot. Landed myself as the wife of one of the richest men in the entire Straits, if not the richest!

I was born in a sleepy town near Slim River, Perak, a one-horse town where, in the blink of an eye, you've passed through. Even the mongrels lounging in the streets were too lazy and scrawny to bark at strangers.

My mother was a cabaret girl, I never knew who my father was. Neither did my mother. From young, I loved watching my mother dress up in sequined cheongsams, coiffuring her long hair into ornate hairdos with glittering ornaments and feathers, putting on her makeup. I observed with a child's curiosity how she pinched her cheeks to make them redder, how she laid on the mascara, the way she donned her silk stockings and slipped into her stiletto heels.

Often, she would bring me along to her workplace, the Pink Flamingo Cabaret in Ipoh, the booming capital of tin-rich Perak. I would sneak out of her dressing room and peep behind the curtains at the world of the cabaret. Rich tycoons with cigars in their mouths and fat wallets in their pockets, laughing women clinging onto their arms, songstresses in shimmering costumes with tight fitting bodices, non-stop music from a live band, waitresses in clingy cheongsams with slits to their thighs, curvaceous *ronggeng* girls in figure-hugging sarong kebayas, the clink of crystal glasses and the pop of champagne bottles, drunken brawls and spats, the smell of money, lots and lots of it. A glittering world of music, glamour and wealth I yearned to be part of. It all revolves around money, my mother said, don't for a minute think it's for the fun of it.

My mother died young. She became a mistress to a Mr Pang, a filthy-rich businessman she met at the cabaret. He provided very well for her and set her up in a shophouse in Concubine Lane, a narrow street in Ipoh where rich tycoons stashed away their mistresses like hidden jewels for secret trysts. She liked him a lot and looked forward to his visits. But she became very bored with her life as a mistress. She missed the cabaret, the glamour, the attention lavished on her by her admirers, the bohemian life.

As a mistress, all her time was spent doing nothing except trying to look desirable against the onslaughts of age, waiting for her lover's visits which were few and rare. She began to gamble to pass the time. It became a full blown obsession and she was bad at it. She gambled away all his money then pawned away her jewellery, even her clothes.

The more she lost the more she took to drink – whisky, vodka and XO, which she drank neat. Her looks faded, she became unkempt and haggard, reeking of alcohol. It came as no surprise when Sugar Daddy decided to dump her. Gangsters came one night and threw my mother and I out of the house and locked us out.

She became a street walker, plying her business in the side roads near Concubine Lane. Whenever she had a customer, she would push me into the cupboard in the dingy room she rented and tell me to go to sleep till her 'business' was over. She died shortly after, shrivelled and yellow from liver failure.

I did not know who to go to so I returned to the only

place I was familiar with – the Pink Flamingo Cabaret. I had just turned fourteen and was aware of my looks from the way men stared at me. The owner hired me on the spot as a dance hostess, making me wear thick makeup to disguise my age. He ogled me and exclaimed, "Pity about your mother... but my, my, she's passed on her good looks to you. You, my child, have a very bright future here."

I continued my training in the art of flirtation and seduction from the senior cabaret ladies. They taught me a thing or two... how to massage a man, how to play helpless and arouse a man's protective instincts, how to speak as if the words are caressing him, how to switch on the tear ducts, how to use body language to tantalise.

My main aim in life was to get a very rich man to support me. A mistress could get dumped anytime; being a wife was a safer bet. No millionaire or millionaire's son from a good family would marry me with my background. But I knew how to make men go weak at their knees.

That's exactly what I did when I met this distinguished gentleman, Mr Gan, who dropped by at the Pink Flamingo one night accompanied by his business partners. His entrance created a stir of excitement, I overheard whispers that here was one of the richest man in the Straits. This was my chance. I used every trick I knew.

Wife Number Two
Wife Number Three sickening, want Baba Gan all the time pay attention to her. Never help with housework,

order everyone about all the time. I very fed up. First Black Face order me do this do that, and now Painted Face also! When no one looking, Painted Face pinch me till blue black, call me bad words sound like people private parts. When Baba Gan around, she sweet like angel, so sweet want to vomit.

But hahaha I the only one who give Baba Gan sons. Number One cannot and Number Three forever trying.

Wife Number Three
I knew Baba Gan was rich but I didn't know I had struck a goldmine! This mansion is like a palace compared to my dingy ratty room. I am waited upon by a whole retinue of servants, cooks, butlers, slave girls. I have to sniff out who I can use as my spies. My husband's siblings, in-laws, aunts and uncles drop by far too often to visit. They give me dirty looks and think I am a gold-digger.

The two wives are no competition at all. Number Two is a stupid fat toad. But she is very fertile and can produce sons like a rambutan tree forever in season – that could be a problem. It is Wife Number One who is the real enemy. Too clever for my liking. She keeps the household running like a well-oiled machine, nothing misses her eagle eye. However, I can see inside her head – she hates me and is scheming away underneath that old-fashioned *sanggul* of hers.

She is much older than me. She should be thankful I attend to her husband's needs, gives her more time for her gambling surely. She is getting creaky and wrinkly and has backache problems. Her time is past. I will become the real mistress of this mansion.

Wife Number One

I was against this polygamy thing from the start. Now it looks like I have to resort to it to fight back. Wife Number Three has Baba Gan eating off her fingers. No fool like an old fool!

Beauty is brief and doesn't last. Her looks will wither too. When there are plenty of dishes on the menu, why keep to the same old dish, especially a wealthy man like my husband who has such an enormous appetite? I will wait patiently and strike when the time is right.

In the kitchen there is a very young girl, just a child. She was born in the servants' quarters more than twelve years ago, the illegitimate child of one of the *mui tsai*, a slave girl my husband Baba Gan inherited in one of his poker sessions. This *mui tsai* begged me to let her keep her baby daughter when she was born. I refused – an extra mouth to feed and an unnecessary distraction. She grovelled and begged, promising me her little girl would serve me her entire lifetime if I could just let her keep her baby.

The *mui tsai*... what's-her-name I can't remember... almost berserk with grief, wrapped herself around my knees, pleading with all her might. The baby gurgled and looked very endearing. I found myself giving in to the *mui tsai*. It did mean an extra helping hand once the child grew up, but she would be forever indebted to me along with her mother.

Now, to everyone's astonishment, this child has grown

into an exquisite creature, the most beautiful thing with a golden complexion, light brown eyes, long wavy tresses. A little *chap cheng* child, God knows who her father is. She strikes me as quite intelligent too. I learnt from the servants her name is Cantik.

I have been whispering into the child's ear at every opportunity I get that I will lift her out of her bondage. She looks puzzled, smiles innocently out of gratitude. She will find out soon my plans for her.

Baba Gan now spends Monday nights with me after my incessant complaints. Tuesday night he's with Number Two and the rest of the week, he is with Number Three. He is usually tired out by the end of the week, not surprisingly, and sleeps a lot on Mondays.

Tomorrow is Monday, my turn... we shall see if he sleeps throughout. We shall see.

Wife Number Three

I am terribly excited. Baba Gan has to make a trip to London next year to receive an award at the Court of Saint James. He hasn't said yet who he'll bring along. Wife Number One is a dreary sourpuss, Number Two no need to even discuss. I know how to enjoy life and enjoy money, what better companion than me? If he chooses to bring that dour first wife instead of me, he will be sorry. I won't speak nor make love to him for a long, long time.

Wife Number One

On Monday night, Baba Gan crawls grumpily into bed without even looking at me. I try to talk to him to revive some semblance of the friendship we once shared. But ever since that scheming Loo Loo came into the picture, he is totally disinterested. He crawls into bed, switches off the lights and goes to sleep.

I lie there quietly for a while, trying not to succumb to self-pity. It is time to act. I slip out of the room, run over to the next room where the little child slave, Cantik, is waiting for me dressed in nothing but a sarong wrapped around her. She looks confused and is trembling with fear.

I grab her by the wrist and drag her to the master bedroom. She struggles in panic but I clench her wrist fiercely and pinch her. She gasps in pain. I whisper urgently into her ear, "You will have a good life, a far better life, no more a slave. Do you understand? Just obey my orders."

Tears well up in her eyes as she nods and bows her head. I open the door of the master bedroom and shove her in. I announce in a loud voice, "Here, my husband, I have a new toy for you. She is a young slave girl, the child of the *mui tsai* you brought home many years ago. You can have this sweet, innocent thing for your pleasure. I will even agree if you want to have her as your Wife Number Four."

I slam the door shut and using the heavy brass key, lock the door of the room. Cantik cannot escape now, even if she were to change her mind. Neither can he, not that he will want to.

I hear some shuffling, struggling, a muffled scream. After a while, all is quiet and still from behind the locked door. It is now my turn to smirk with pleasure. I think soon... very soon... there will be a Wife Number Four. I will happily drink that cup of tea at the wedding ceremony of Baba Gan and Wife Number Four!

Chong lai chong kee
Meaning: To rush from one place to another
to complete particular tasks

M chai si
Meaning: Foolhardy, throwing caution to the wind

Bo ha mih ua ho kong
Meaning: Nothing much to say

Tan Siew Imm, *Penang Hokkien-English Dictionary*

Beaded nyonya shoes, also called kasut manek

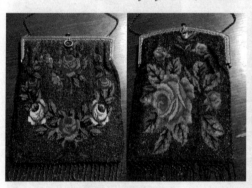

Beaded evening bags
(Images courtesy Mr & Mrs Tye Soon Ping)

Open-toed kasut manek, *called* muka chakiak, *named after Chinese wooden clogs*

Beaded evening bags
(Image courtesy Dr Harriet Wong)

*Beaded panel of two peacocks done in
semi-pointillist style
(Image courtesy Ken Yap)*

*Antique Nyonya beaded slippers
(Images courtesy Mr & Mrs Tye Soon Ping)*

The Kueh Brothers

This will teach Big Bully a lesson, calling me 'Fatty Bom Bom'. I'm now a businessman. And I'm only 10 years old.

"Oh yeah, and what business izzit?" Big Bully asks with that stupid grin. I push out my chest like a cat facing an enemy.

"I sell cakes. A cake businessman!" I smirk.

"Hahaha," he hoots, slapping his forehead, his bunch of nincompoop mates giggling along.

"Cakes? Did you hear that, fellas? Hee hee... that's for sissies! Like you!" He shoves me in the chest. I fall splat on the muddy ground.

My big brother, Khee, shows up just in time. Big Bully and his gang run like crazy, mocking, *"Fatty Fatty Bom Bom, Curi curi jagong, Fatty Fatty Bom Bom, Curi curi jagong."*

My brother pulls me up from the mud, puts his arm around me. "Next time that idiot *kachau* you, I will punch his bulldog face."

He's two years older than me, but my Ko, which means Big Brother, is tough and street-smart and my hero.

Making cakes may be a girly thing, but I don't *make* the cakes. I *sell* them all day long, six times a week. My mother is the one who makes the cakes; my brother and I have been given the very important job of selling them. Very dangerous, as boys can get snatched off the streets and forced into labour gangs. Pa says it's safe, they are only interested in males between sixteen to fifty years of age. Pa gives us his gigantic Raleigh bicycle to use. My feet can't even reach the pedals; Ko's feet just about touches them. I get to sit behind and hold the baskets of cakes.

Ma says they're called *kueh*, not cakes. She is famous for her *nyonya kueh*. She comes from a Penang family which makes the best *kueh* in the world. When Pa lost his job and all his properties were grabbed by those nasty fellas in uniforms, we were in big trouble. Ma looked out of her kitchen window at the coconut trees and chickens pecking away, and came up with the idea of making *nyonya kueh*. Her *nyonya kueh* business has been good and is keeping us alive.

We are now a bulging, expanding family from an initial family of parents, three daughters and Ko and me. Relatives keep turning up at our doorstep, and my parents keep taking them in. My sisters are not pleased. I don't know why – they have strict orders to hide in the attic so they don't need much space. Our house is a spacious wooden bungalow with lots of rooms and a compound full of coconut and fruit trees. Our relatives think they will be fine here but the truth is, we are always hungry.

Of the many 'hangers-on', as Eldest Sister calls them,

I like Ah Gow Chee, she's always calm and kind, never an unkind word from her. She lost her entire family in a bomb attack. Pek Nya Chee and Bersak Chee, Ma's cousins, are stuck here too, all because they came to Kuala Lumpur to shop at Robinsons.

Pek Nya Chee grumbles every day, longing to return to Penang. In the evenings she rolls out a mat at the front hall, kneels down and chants in a strange language, knocking her head on the floor over and over. After a while, she pulls herself up, groaning about her lousy knees, fastens her sarong and waddles into the kitchen. Her dainty sister, Bersak Chee, prays every day too, crossing herself and muttering Hail Marys. Ma told us she was in love with an English army officer but her parents objected. She gave in to her parents but refused to marry for the rest of her life after that. She's like a sparrow, demure with soft candy floss silver hair. Her eyes look sad even when she smiles. Ko and I have to give up our room to them. We like camping out in the front hall, just like the Boy Scouts.

A few weeks later, another relative shows up, Ma's loud uncle, Orr Kow, which means black dog in Hokkien. He has an opinion on everything which drives Pa nuts. Ma says Black Dog didn't even pass his Standard Six. He has a twin brother, Pek Kow (white dog) back home. When they were born, their parents, worried jealous evil spirits would harm the twins, gave them crummy names to appease the spirits. Ma says the two brothers fight a lot but are inseparable. Orr Kow won't tell us how he got parted from his brother.

A funny looking lady holding a candy-pink umbrella knocks on our door one afternoon. She's in a white cheongsam, with two slits revealing spidery blue veins on her white thighs. She has lots of makeup on, her eyebrows look like thin question marks and her hair is piled on top of her head. Two big leather suitcases squat like unwanted guests beside her.

"Good morning. Is there anybody home?" she calls out in very good English.

Pa cringes when he looks out of the window,

"*Alamak*, Molek Ee is outside the door!" he exclaims in dismay. "Just how many more relatives do you have?"

"Molek Ee? That bossy vainpot? Cham, *arn chua ho*? We can't turn her away. Her grandfather was kind to my family," Ma whispers to Pa.

We all groan. Ma gives us a look which shuts us up instantly.

"Hellooo. *Anybudee*? Surely there must be *somebudee* home," rings Molek Ee's sharp voice.

It takes a few minutes to unlock the door. Molek Ee switches from her high-class English into Hokkien, beads of sweat glistening on her forehead.

"*Aiyahhhh... hamisoo uh-nae koo-eh? Chincha juak! Juak ka beh see! Ka kwai lah, eh sei wor?*"

Ma told us later Molek Ee was very beautiful in her younger days, pursued by countless suitors, but she was so fussy and picky she scorned them all, waiting for the biggest catch to turn up. Years later, she had become too old for the marriage market. Now, in her late sixties, she looks like a bride in waiting, face powdered white, lips gaudy red, all dressed up but nowhere to go.

"Psssssst, mutton-dressed-as-lamb coming!" Orr Kow mutters when she enters the room, dressed up in weird outfits every time.

Bersak Chee suppresses giggles while Ah Gow Chee frowns at him.

Molek Ee, haughty and snobbish, can't get along with the others, especially Pek Nya Chee who can't stand her patronising ways. They glare and *joo ling* each other and squabble all the time.

"*Siau cha bor kui!*" Pek Nya Chee calls Molek Ee. I was told it means 'mad she-devil'.

"Uncouth bumbling country bumpkin!" Molek Ee calls Pek Nya.

My Hokkien and English improve every day.

Pa's company suddenly shut down when the enemies invaded the country. Pa was furious his English bosses did not warn their local employees but got their families and themselves out of Malaya speedily.

"They could have at least told us the Japs have landed! They never gave us a choice! Basket!" Pa likes to use strange swear words.

"The sun will never set on the empire... well, it's gone!

The mighty British Empire has fallen. It's every man for himself now," he tells us grimly one evening.

He warns, "I may get arrested. I need to prepare you all for that."

Ma clutches her throat in fear.

"You boys...you two young men... have to take care of everyone here if I"m taken away," Pa says turning to my brother and me.

My brother braces his shoulders trying to look like a man. I follow Ko.

"How long these *seelangjeepoonakui* going to be around? *Basket*!" I swear like Pa.

"*Siau-ah?* Don't you dare call them that! I will wash your mouth with chilli!" Ma snaps at me, "and how dare you swear!"

Oww, she's done that before, spicy-hot-blinking-painful. Ma is very strict and always punishes in twos – both my brother and I get it no matter who's wrong. I am about to tell Ma I learnt that '*seelang* dead devil' word from her but my brother gives me that '*shaddup*, you stupid' look.

"Yes Ma," I say meekly instead.

Ma's the one who told me it was rude to call people names. "Sticks and stones may break my bones but names will never hurt me," was what she taught me to say if Big Bully calls me names. Before Fatty Bom Bom, it was Botak Head. Ma found *kutu*, itchy tiny lice, in my hair one morning and shaved Ko and me completely bald.

Everybody is nervous and jittery nowadays. Pa hides in his room or slips out. To where, he won't say. Ko thinks Pa is working with something resisting. I don't know what he's resisting as the Japs are already here. Once I saw Pa taking out the radio – from the rice bin of all places, then he locks himself in his room. I ask him later why so secretive and he tells me sternly, "Don't tell anyone. Ever! On pain of death, you hear me?"

I'm not sure what he means.

"Pa, is it still painful if we're dead?"

Pa doesn't respond, his forehead all crinkled up with worry.

"We're running out of rice, Pa, better hide the radio somewhere else," I tell him.

"Clever boy," Pa pats my head and smiles his kindly smile, which I miss a lot.

I think Pa is worried because we are starving. And we are all sick of tapioca. *Ubi kayu* for breakfast, lunch and dinner every day! For breakfast, it's *pok chan* – tapioca mashed, flattened, steamed and served as pancakes. But it's still *ubi kayu* in a different shape. Sometimes, Ma makes another dish, *ragee*, from the seeds of a type of grass. My aunts grind the seeds into flour then steam the horrid bitter paste. We look evil after swallowing the vile thing, our mouths and tongues coated in black.

Everything we took for granted before – rice, sugar, salt,

cooking oil, bread, soap, medicines – has to be bought in the black market. Any little item will fetch some money, even a fountain pen can feed a family for two days. Pa manages to make a bit of money buying and selling cigarettes. We learn to make do with the little we have. We brush our teeth with salt or finely ground charcoal, and chew coconut twigs as a sort of toothbrush. Our clothes are turning into rags.

One day, I dress up like a Japanese soldier, a plastic sword around my waist and Pa's cap with a hanky tied at the back as a flap on my head. Ma almost faints when she sees me.

"*Lu siau ah?* Gone mad? Take it off!" she grabs me and pinches me hard.

Owww, no wonder Pa calls her *cili padi*, terror fierce one... pain like anything. My arm is blue-black for days.

Ma destroyed everything in the house that reminded her of the Japanese. Even a picture of a snowy mountain from a calendar and my sister's doll in a kimono. Ma is not the same after they chopped off her brother's head because he would not bow to their flag. No one dared get his head back stuck on a spike at their headquarters. Ma has trouble sleeping – says she sees her brother crying, wants his head back and cannot rest in peace. I get nightmares of Uncle Eng Kiat, a rotting, headless stump crawling with maggots. He used to make us roll with laughter with his *fei tai saw* stories, the adventures of a big fat buffoon always getting into trouble.

Our *kueh* business starts at 5.30 am every day. Eldest Sister collects eggs from the chicken coop, pandan and banana leaves from the garden and blue pea flowers growing wild over the fence. Second Sister grates the pile of coconuts using a metal scraper attached to a wooden stool. Third Sister and my aunts prepare the glutinous rice, gula melaka, the leaves for wrapping and extract santan. Ma mixes the various ingredients to make the *kueh* which are then steamed or baked. Then they are cut into dainty diamond shapes or wrapped in banana leaves and placed in the baskets for sale. Ma comes to wake up my brother and me.

"Oww, I want to sleep some more," mumbles Ko, "just a bit more, Ma."

"Ma, five more minutes okay? Just five more minutes please," I plead, my eyes refusing to open.

"Get up, wash up, get dressed! No bargaining and hurry up !" Ma commands.

Ma is fierce and businesslike, ordering everyone around. Orr Kow calls her Sergeant-Major. She used to smile lots more in the past but now she works and works all the time and looks and sounds like an angry tiger.

Waking up to the smell of the *kueh* is heavenly. All my favourite smells – fresh coconut, *gula melaka*, caramelised bananas – drive me crazy, especially when I can't eat them. They're all strictly for sale. Ma makes many kinds of *kueh: kueh koci, kueh talam, abok abok, onde onde, pulut inti, kueh lapis, kueh seri muka.* My favourite is *pulut tai tai,* a gorgeous blue *kueh* served with kaya, a delicious coconut-egg jam. That's when I can't resist begging Ma for a slice. Sometimes she gives me one out of pity. My sisters say it's to shut me up.

There's one *kueh* which Ma isn't too good at. A nyonya named Seh Han Ee makes the best *huat kueh* in the whole of KL. *Huat kueh* are rice cupcakes made of coconut water, rice flour and toddy, steamed over high heat. A good *huat kueh* is one that has risen nicely with a crack at the top. Seh Han Ee's *huat kueh* is soft and fluffy with the perfect finish. She guards her recipe very carefully but Ma has her ways and means. She gives Ko some money and sends us to buy a *huat kueh* from Seh Han Eee undercover.

When we return, Ma analyses it like a science experiment. She breaks it into half, studies it, pulls it apart, tastes it carefully. She sends us to the toddy shop to buy toddy – a vital ingredient for *huat kueh.* She gives us two empty bottles, tossing some flour inside. If we get stopped by the police, we are to say we're buying toddy for our mother to make *kueh;* we are not toddy addicts. The flour acts as proof. Ma's clever like that, she always thinks ahead.

Luckily, no one stops us. Once we're back with the toddy, she sets about making *huat kueh.* When they're ready, Ma is overjoyed – she has nailed it! The colourful pink and white cakes have cracked prettily and taste delicious. Pek Nya Chee exclaims, "*Ho chiak, ho chiak,*" and Orr Kow takes one bite and declares, "Sergeant-Major, I salute you." Ah Gow

Chee pays the biggest compliment when she says, "It's even better than the original."

I have not seen Ma smile for a long time. Molek Ee, of course, irritates everyone when she reminds my mother, "Imitation is the best form of flattery."

My brother and I roam all over KL selling the *kueh*. Sometimes Bukit Bintang or Imbi Road near our house on Treacher Road. Sometimes we go to Pudu Road, Shaw Road, Jalan Kia Peng or as far as Ampang. Eldest Sister told us to sing, "*Kueh kueh, Nyonya kueh*" as our signature tune. We are shy at first, mumbling "*kueh kueh*" under our breath especially when there are people around. But there's Ma's anger if we return with the *kueh* unsold so we get louder and better and our *kueh* sell like hot cakes.

Molek Ee says sending out two little boys to sell *kueh* is like "feeding them to the lions". Too risky, we will get cheated, robbed. Well, no one cheats us. We meet some really kind people. One elderly lady on Imbi road, Aunty Siew Keen Chee, is very kind. She comes out from her cosy bungalow to buy *kueh* from us every day although she too has fallen on hard times. Even when she has no money, she will pick a few *kueh*, promising to pay later. Ma is quite sure her old friend is helping us out in this way.

Our favourite haunt is Conlay Road, where the *ho gyak lang*, or rich folks, live in large houses with beautiful lawns surrounded by shady trees. Here lives another kind couple, a lawyer and his wife, Ah Bok Koh and Ah Bok Soh, Pa's friends. Ko and I used to play badminton with their sons. Their boys teach us how to find food in an ingenious way as we are perennially hungry. First, we scatter some rice grains onto the dining table to lure the sparrows while we hide behind the doors. When the sparrows fly in through the French windows and are pecking away, we quietly shut all the windows. Using our badminton rackets we swat them like flies, then boil them up in a pot with the rice grains and water. Sparrow *chok* or porridge is simply delicious. The skinny sparrows don't have much meat but with every mouthful, they taste like fat juicy chicken in our starving minds.

There's one place where our *kueh* sell out fast, somewhere near Circular Road. Our calls of *kueh* bring out a number of heavily-painted young women who don't have many clothes on. They're not shy about it too. They smell of perfume and flowers and have coloured toe- and finger nails. Ko says they are 'whores', doing business just like us. I don't know what they're selling as I'm always busy trying to fight them off. They love to pat our botak heads, tug at our trousers or try to hug or kiss us. Sometimes when they're drunk, they behave crazily, chasing us round and round, grabbing our baskets of *kueh*, screaming with laughter when we chase them in return to get our baskets back. Maybe they miss playing with children. We don't see any children there. Not once did they cheat – they always pay for their *kueh*.

One late afternoon, we return home tired out to a house full of howling, weeping women. My sisters are sobbing in the front hall. A chair lies overturned and there's broken glass and cigarette butts on the floor. Pek Nya Chee is wailing and beating her chest, Bersak Chee and Ah Gow Chee look shaken trying to calm her. Even Molek Ee's face has turned a paler shade of white.

"Where's Pa and Ma?"

Orr Kow points to the bedroom, growling, unable to speak for once.

We find Ma there. Alone. My legs turn soft like jelly.

I start crying, "Where's Pa? Where's Pa?"

Ko tries to act calm, "Ma, are you alright? Where is Pa?"

Ma's face is streaked with tears and her whole body is shivering. She looks about to collapse but she's forcing herself to remain calm, rummaging through documents in the cupboard.

"Your father has been taken away. They arrested him an hour ago. Someone betrayed him."

Then after a long pause, Ma announces in a voice of steel, "Tomorrow we will make *assam laksa*."

Why is Ma thinking of food at this terrible time?

"We have to earn more money. *Assam laksa* will bring in a lot more money. Pa gave me the names of some contacts, we will use the money to secure Pa's release."

"Get moving, no more sitting around wallowing in tears.

Pa is not dead yet. Bribery may yet work."

We are thankful Ma's given us something to hold on to, to hope for. Ma is back in army commander mode, barking orders at everyone.

The next morning, Ma and her team of helpers make a huge pot of *assam laksa* soup. *Assam laksa* is a delicious spicy-hot-sour fish soup served with noodles, garnished with onions, pineapple, mint and other veggies. Ma likes to use *ikan parang* for her *assam laksa* but with no fish available, she resorts to sardines from the black market. They have spent hours preparing the noodles, the garnishing and the soup. Instead of bantering and bickering, everyone is quiet and solemn, worried about Pa, trapped in their own fears.

When the *assam laksa* is ready, my sisters help Ma to hang the pot of steaming hot soup on the handlebar of the bicycle. Ko clasps the handle of the pot along with the handlebar of the bicycle in one tight grip. I am seated at the back clutching the baskets of *kueh* and *assam laksa* garnishing. Ko's cycling has improved but it is still pretty difficult balancing a huge pot of soup and a passenger on a bicycle. So far so good, he is cycling along steadily and we are doing fine heading for Imbi Road.

Until he decides to take a short cut across a narrow wooden bridge somewhere along Bukit Bintang Road.

"Er... maybe we should get off and walk across," I suggest.

"No *lah*. It's hard to get back on the bike. Just sit still and hold tight."

As we cross the bridge, Ko's cycling gets a little wobbly.

"Cannot, cannot *lah, beh sai, beh sai*," I mutter in fright.

Ko says, "*Eh sai, eh sai*, can can."

The bicycle wobbles violently and topples over. We fall off along with the pot of soup and the baskets.

Ko and I are sprawled on the ground, Ko yelping in pain, his left leg scalded by the hot soup. I am stunned, dripping with cucumber, onion and chilli. The noodles are scattered all over the ground.

"We can always wash them, no one will know," I'm desperate.

"No, we can't. You need soup for *assam laksa* and that's all gone."

The precious soup is splattered all over the ground. Even the *kueh* cannot be recycled, covered in dirt. We pick up the bicycle, the baskets and the empty pot and crawl under the bridge in shame. We are terrified.

"This time we are going to *kena* from Ma," I mumble, "we're really going to get it!"

"Yes, we are really in hot soup," says Ko, using an idiom from Molek Ee.

I cannot even manage a smile, thinking only of the *rotan*, a long thin rattan cane which Ma uses to punish us when we misbehave.

"I bet you she will use the *rotan* this time," I moan.

Ko bites his lower lip which is beginning to quiver,

trying hard to be his usual tough self. I pretend not to notice.

"Hey Ko, I have two exercise books hidden under my bed. Put one under your pants, the caning won't hurt."

"I'm not thinking about the *rotan*," Ko is in tears, "It's Pa. Every minute counts, every sen and dollar counts. And what have we done? Dropped the whole pot! Lost all that money! Let Ma and everybody down!"

We sit for a long time under the bridge sobbing and sniffling. Deep inside, we are terrified at the thought of losing Pa. Will he lose his head like Uncle Eng Kiat? Pa is a strong guy, another hero like my Ko. He has a black belt in judo and knows how to tie and untie all sorts of knots. There are trophies in his library for long distance running in his school days. He knows some Japanese words too – maybe he could talk his way out or kick or fight his way out. I cannot imagine life without him. I want Pa back desperately.

Ko and I crawl out from under the bridge. We cycle around for hours, too scared to go home. We are bruised, scalded, shivering with hunger. We try to kill time loitering around the shops but become a nuisance with no money to spend. Ko cycles to the railway track near Davidson Road. We hang around there playing on the track, trying to trap birds with the empty baskets. Dangling green mangoes tempt us; I stand on Ko's shoulders and swipe one – it tastes raw and sour. It's twilight now and we are still frightened and ashamed to face Ma. When it gets really dark, sick of being bitten by mosquitoes, we finally head home on the squeaking, dented bicycle.

There's a commotion in the house again. Everyone is in a state of panic. My sisters are weeping and sobbing in the hall but scream in joy when they see us. Ma and our relatives are missing. Eldest Sister says they've gone out to look for us.

An hour later, Ma returns home with the search party.

When she see us, she yells in absolute fury, "Don't you ever do it again! How dare you! Never, ever do that again!"

She marches towards us, her face scrunched up in anger. We tremble in fear.

"It was an... an accident," Ko stutters, "Ma, I'm... we're sorry... I tried to cross the brr... bb.. bridge, I wanted to save ttt.. time..."

Ma stuns us by going down on her knees and sweeping us into her arms. She hugs us so tightly I can hardly breathe. I have almost forgotten how her touch feels like. I want her to hold me like this for a long, long time. She holds us close as if she doesn't ever want to let go.

Ma finally releases us and cries, "I don't mean the *assam laksa*, you idiots ! I mean you two. Don't you dare disappear on me! You made me go crazy with worry. I lost your father yesterday. Do you want me to lose my sons as well? *Siau ah?*"

Her words spill out in a torrent of relief. Looking exhausted, she gets up onto her feet again and says firmly, "We'll get through this. We'll get Pa back. We'll beat these *seelangjeepoonakui*. Just you wait and see. Now get to work, everybody! Start peeling the onions. Tomorrow we make *assam laksa* again!"

HOAY KIM CHNEH

Rhyme	Translation
Hoay Kim Chneh,	Fireflies!
Chap Goh Meh,	Fifteenth Night!
Chnia Lu Eh Ku Wa,	Invite your brothers-in-law,
Lai Chiak Teh	To drink tea,
Teh Sio Sio,	If the tea is too hot.
Kia Lor Bey Kin Chio,	Take a stroll to buy bananas,
Kin Chio Bey Khi Pek,	If you forget to peel the bananas,
Kia Lor Bey Chek,	Take a stroll to buy a book,
Chek Bey Khi Thak,	If you forget to read the book,
Kia Lor Bey Bak,	Take a stroll to buy ink stick,
Bak Bey Khi Bua,	If you forget to grind the ink stick,
Kia Lor Bey Chua,	Take a stroll to buy a snake,
Chua Bey Khi Liak,	If you forget to catch the snake,
Kia Lor Bey Khar Kiak,	Take a stroll to buy wooden clogs,
Khar Kiak Bey Khi Cheng,	If you forget to wear the wooden clogs,
Kia Lor Bey Kar Leng,	Take a stroll to buy mynah birds,
Kar Leng Koe,	Male mynah,
Kar Leng Soh,	Female mynah,
Ch'nia Lu Eh Ku Wa,	Invite your brothers-in-law,
Sio Ean Toh!	To a wrestling match!

Raymond Kwok, *Hokkien Rhymes and Ditties*

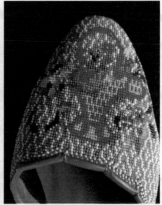

Beaded shoes with basket motif

*Motif of two young boys on a
kamcheng cover
(Image courtesy Ken Yap)*

*Tudong saji or food cover with beaded top
(Image courtesy Peter Wee)*

*A tengkat or tiffin carrier
(Image courtesy Peter Wee)*

Mould used for making top hats

Enamel trays used for drying flour
or dry ingredients

Kueh bangkit moulds

Pestle and mortar

Antique porcelain jelly mould

Jelly moulds in animal shapes

Green Eyes

When Gin Leng read about her in the newspapers, he had to steady himself for a moment. His head spun. He could not believe his eyes. But... but she was dead. She never came home. There had been no contact at all for years. Not a word for fifty years.

That unmistakable name, Jacquelina. There was a press photograph of her – angry and tense, standing with a cluster of women dressed in *hanboks*, the Korean traditional costume, a few holding placards, waving fists angrily in the air. Her arms were crossed against her chest in a posture of defiance. She had the same sharp features, the slightly tilted nose, the broad shoulders. Her eyes, though, were hidden behind large sunglasses, those amazing unforgettable eyes that seemed to look right into your soul.

Not a day had passed when he did not think of her, wondering what had happened to her since that fateful night. Her piercing screams have haunted him all his life, invading his dreams, tormenting him for years. He was certain the woman in the press article was the girl he loved dearly in the past. The cause she was fighting for made him shudder with revulsion and horror. He wanted to forget, delete the memory of her forever, but he could not.

He had to find her.

"It's her! It's Jacq, guys," he yelled.

Jacquelina Cordeiro was his childhood friend. It started out that way. She was the younger sister of his best friend, Jacob, from the only Eurasian family living in his neighbourhood. Gin Leng and Jacob were part of a gang called the Fearless Five. Gin Leng, the gang leader, wasn't keen to have Jacquelina in their all-boys gang at first, but as she tagged along everywhere with her brother, he didn't have much choice. Jacob would have pulled out if they didn't include her. Jacob was very protective of her, especially after their mother suddenly passed away. The rest of the gang, Bertie, Siew Wai and Nick, didn't mind as long as she wasn't a nuisance.

She was brave and gutsy, joining headlong in all their activities. She proved herself their equal for she could outrun and out-cycle them, participating ably in all their games. In soccer, she awed them by the artful way she dribbled the ball and her ballet-like twirls. Dressed in scruffy pants and old T-shirts, her wavy hair tucked under a cap, she looked and behaved just like one of them. A joyful, cheeky and spontaneous person, she was great fun to be with. The boys accepted her as one of them and called her Jacq.

One thing she could do which the boys couldn't was to play the piano beautifully. Her mother, a music teacher, had passed on her love of music to Jacq. She was a natural when her fingers touched the ivory keys, playing by ear, transported into a beautiful imaginary world. Another distinctive feature was the unusual colour of her eyes. They were an amazing green, the colour of rock pools in mysterious limestone caves explorers stumble upon and gasp for their sheer beauty. Jacq's alluring eyes changed with the light and her moods – soft transparent green in the sunshine, emerald in her brooding, dark moods.

"I wish I could paint them black", she confided in Gin Leng once.

They were sitting on the edge of the floor of the tree house eating rambutans. Gin Leng's father, Baba Teoh Hock Guan, a schoolteacher, skilled in carpentry, had built an impressive tree house up in the rambutan tree in the backyard.

"I'm sick and tired of people asking me about my green eyes."

"Why are they like that?"

"What? The people?"

"No. Your eyes? Why are they green?"

"You too!" she laughed throwing her head back, swinging her legs dangerously in the air.

"Watch out, girl. Don't fall over!"

"Don't call me Girl."

"Sit back a little further, Jacq, please. You're too close to the edge."

She obeyed, but not before reaching out precariously to grab a few more rambutans from a nearby branch.

"So why?"

"So why what?" she looked up at him quizzically, momentarily distracted, the juice of the luscious sweet fruit dribbling down one side of her mouth which she licked away.

"Why are your eyes so green?"

"Oh, that. My grandmother Marguerite. I take after her. That's what Mummy told me. She was born in the Netherlands, a Dutch woman who came over to the Dutch East Indies in the last century. They settled in Batavia and lived a grand lifestyle over there. Her father became a very wealthy man and owned numerous plantations in Java and Sumatra.

"Your grandmother was from Europe?"

"Yes, but she loved the East. She fell in love with a Javanese musician from Solo, a vocalist in the kerontjong band she met on chap goh meh. My mother is the youngest of their three children. Mummy says Marguerite had green eyes, brown hair and was very fair."

"I've never met her, she died young. All the women in my family seem to die young," Jacq continued, her eyes turning darkish green.

"They're... very beautiful. When you grow up, those eyes will break a lot of mens' hearts," he teased.

"Really?" she asked wide-eyed, "Will they break yours?"

That question so jolted him he almost fell off the tree house.

When she turned thirteen, Jacq was perturbed at the physical changes to her body. With no mother to guide her, she was a little lost as she blossomed into a lovely young girl. All the physical activity out in the sun gave her a strong toned physique and her fair skin a golden tan. Her body developed curves, her hair grew lustrous and thick. She became self-conscious when she was with the gang, especially when she started shooting up taller than them. Her curvaceous figure began to show through her shapeless garments.

The first time she wore a dress was when Aunt Matilda came to stay and cooked a grand feast for Christmas. Aunt Matilda, Jacq's father's unmarried sister, travelled to Kuala Lumpur from Singapore every year to join her brother for the Christmas family reunion. Matilda was a superb cook and baker. Her Christmas fruit cake and sugee cake could reduce one to whimpers at first bite, and her Devil curry seared itself into one's memory at first taste. Gin Leng and his parents and the rest of the gang were invited over to Jacob and Jacq's home for Christmas lunch that year.

The Cordeiro house was all dressed up with silver candles, red and green ribbons and a Christmas tree in the corner of the living room, festooned in baubles and glitter. Posies of colourful fresh flowers in glass bottles adorned the window sills. Jacq's father, a well-known doctor, welcomed them warmly into the cosy lounge. While Dr Cordeiro chatted amiably with Gin Leng's parents and Matilda ran in and out of the kitchen, fussing over the table presentation and checking on the huge bird roasting in the oven,

Gin Leng and the boys, squeezed together into the huge sofa, fidgeted and teased each other. Jacq was nowhere to be seen.

"Where's Jacq?" the boys asked Jacob.

"She went upstairs to change."

"Why?"

"Because Aunt Matilda asked Jacq to wear the Christmas present she got for her."

"What is it?"

"A dress. Something Jacq detests wearing but she didn't want to hurt Aunty's feelings. Don't know why she's taking so long."

Just then, Gin Leng, seated right across the staircase, saw a pair of shapely legs and slim ankles descend hesitantly down the staircase right in front of his eyes. He muttered aloud, "Wow!"

All heads turned as Jacq came down the stairs in a lacy white dress, looking sheepish, almost apologetic. She took everyone's breath away with her fresh, stunning beauty. Her long wavy hair tumbled down her shoulders. The dress was a little tight around the bodice, pressing against her breasts. Aunt Matilda had underestimated the rate at which her niece was growing.

"Wow, is that really you, Jacq?" teased Siew Wai, "you don't look... er... like yourself."

"Yeah Jacq, you have legs," teased Bertie.

Jacq made grimaces of disgust at them.

"Ooooh, Jacquelina," gasped Aunt Matilda, amazed at the transformation, then nagged her brother.

"You see, my dear Oliver, how pretty your daughter is. You must insist she stops dressing up like a boy."

Dr Cordeiro chuckled, "Aww... it's just a phase she's going through. Give her some time."

His eyes twinkled with pride and adoration at his daughter, struggling to sit down in her uncomfortable flouncy skirt. He gave her a wink and she smiled back, her green eyes impishly mischievous.

Gin Leng could not take his eyes away from her, stealing furtive glances at Jacq seated across the table. He was two years older and beginning to find her increasingly attractive. Their platonic friendship was evolving into something more, something he had never experienced before. He had become acutely aware of the young girl whom he and the gang members had treated as "one of the boys", growing into a rare beauty.

Her Eurasian ancestry gave her an exotic attractiveness with her deep-set eyes, thick eyelashes, dark brown hair and tawny complexion. Her green eyes sparkled under a pair of arched dark eyebrows and her skin glowed in its youthful luminosity. She had forgotten all about the dress now and was enjoying herself, thrilled to have family and good friends all together. He loved the way she threw her head back to laugh as jokes flew across the table. She caught him looking at her and a faint blush crept over her face. She returned his glance for a brief moment then quickly looked away, the fire in her emerald eyes blazing.

When it came time to help clear the dishes from the

dinner table, Gin Leng scrambled to his feet to help Jacq take the dishes to the kitchen sink. In the kitchen, he whispered to Jacq, "Hey Jacq, you look different today," his eyes wide in open admiration, "for the first time in my life... er... I mean, your life, you look like a girl... a real girl."

" Ugh, this horrid frilly thing is just to please my aunt," she said, scrunching her nose in disdain. "And stop calling me a girl. I'm one of you guys, remember?" she reminded him giving him a friendly punch on his arm.

"Owww, you punch... like a boy," he teased. He didn't want to speak too much as his voice was changing. Jacq giggled, "You definitely sound like a girl!"

"It's as your dad put it, a phase I'm going through. I'll get my masculine baritone very soon," he piped, abhorring his capricious voice.

"One can only hope," she teased, her eyes glowing with glee.

As she was about to lift the glass bowl of Christmas Pudding from the kitchen table, Gin Leng caught hold of her hand impulsively, "Truly I mean it. You look beautiful today. The most beautiful girl I have ever seen."

He released her and pretended to avoid another punch. She tossed her head and sauntered out of the kitchen carrying the pudding laden with mixed fruits and nuts, doused with brandy, the shy smile on her lips betrayed the pleasure she found in his compliment.

When Jacq turned sixteen, the friendship between them had grown deeper into a strong romantic attraction, still unspoken, but obvious in the way they looked at each other and in their gestures of affection. The boys teased them mercilessly but both Gin Leng and Jacq feigned innocence. It was obvious to all they cared deeply for each other.

The year was almost coming to a close. 1941 had been a year of deep anxiety – the fear that the war raging in Europe would reach south-east Asia. Japan, a member of the Axis powers, appeared increasingly threatening in its quest for a Greater East Asia Co-Prosperity Sphere. Nick's uncle, a police officer, warned their friends and families to stock up on food. Bertie told the gang his father was convinced his barber was a Japanese spy from the way he eavesdropped surreptitiously on conversations in his little shop, nicking him several times on his chin. Gin Leng's mother studiously sewed her jewellery into the hem of her cotton blouses, worried they may have to evacuate one day.

On 8 December 1941, the Japanese invasion of British Malaya began just after midnight. Japanese troops landed at Sabak Beach near Kota Bahru, Kelantan and began to infiltrate into the rest of the peninsula on foot and by bicycle. The Japanese forces met stiff resistance initially but their superiority in air power, tanks and infantry tactics and the lack of preparedness on the part of the Allies spelt disaster for the Allies. It was all over by mid-February of 1942 when the Allied forces in Singapore surrendered to the Japanese. A world of peace and innocence was completely overturned for

Gin Leng, Jacq and the gang with the Japanese Occupation of Malaya.

With strict orders from their parents to stay within the confines of their homes, the Fearless Five hardly saw each other now. Gin Leng missed Jacq and his friends a lot and their good times together. The gang gradually dissipated with Bertie's family moving away to rural Selangor and Siew Wai shifting to a relative's home near Gopeng, Perak. Only Gin Leng, Nick, and the Cordeiro siblings remained. Dr. Cordeiro made plans to send Jacq safely away from the city where many Japanese troops were garrisoned. As a medical doctor, he had been ordered by the Japanese Kempetai to tend to their casualties in KL and dared not leave. He had contacted a relative working at a tea plantation in the Cameron Highlands and waited anxiously for him to escort Jacq into hiding.

One evening, Gin Leng heard the sound of pebbles hitting against his bedroom window. Peering out, he saw nothing, only the long thin shadows of the palms looming in the garden below. He went downstairs to check and found a note lying on the grass outside. It read,

Meet me now at tree house. Urgent. Jacq

Jacob ran swiftly to his backyard and scrambled up the rope ladder tied to the huge shady tree. There, crouched inside the tree house, was Jacq, looking agitated and nervous.

"Jacq, what are you doing here? It's dangerous to be out."

"Ssshh it's okay. We're up in a tree. I could live here, it's cosy up here," she whispered.

"No, Jacq, it's not safe. What is it you want to tell me?" he urged, his eyes taking her in, she looked enchanting in the fading twilight, her face flushed with excitement.

"I came to say goodbye. I have to leave soon."

"Where are you going?"

"Dad says it's too dangerous to remain here. I'm going to stay with my cousins in the Blue Valley, up in the highlands. Exciting, huh? But I don't really want to go..."

"Jacq, please be careful. If anything should happen to you, I... I cannot bear it."

"I'll be alright, don't worry. You must be careful too. They're kidnapping young men to serve in the labour camps. Dad says they're building a railway line all the way to Burma."

She reached out for his hand to press a gentle goodbye. He leaned over slowly, pulled her to him and kissed her tenderly.

"I love you Jacq. I will find you when the war is over."

It was dark up in the tree house, night was falling fast. Her green eyes glowed like a cat's in the darkness and he yearned to kiss her again.

"You've got to get back home, Jacq," he said instead, worried for her safety.

She whispered softly, "I love you too. Promise you'll get in touch when all this madness is over. Bye, Gin."

Gin Leng watched Jacq scramble down the rope ladder, creep across the backyard and disappear into the night.

At midnight, Gin Leng and his family were awakened by the screeching of tyres and the stomping of boots. They heard loud pounding followed by hoarse guttural shouts. Dogs barked, people stirred from their sleep and neighbours peered out of their windows, wondering whose fate had tangled with the dreaded enemy.

A scream rang out through the night. Gin Leng felt his blood turn cold. It sounded like Jacq. The noise and commotion were coming from right next door. Shouting, sounds of scuffling and things breaking, then two gun shots pierced the air. He could hear Jacq's screams and the crashing of furniture. Gin Leng grabbed his hockey stick and ran downstairs towards the front door. He found his way blocked by his father, his mother looking pale and trembling with fright, standing beside his Pa.

"They've come for Jacq, Pa. I've got to save her. Let me go to her."

"There is nothing you can do. If you run over there, you will be shot dead instantly. Don't do anything stupid," his father said firmly.

"Pa, please. I cannot stand here and do nothing. Please get out of my way."

"They will shoot you on sight! Do you want to be a dead hero?"

His mother, Eng Neo, a gentle, soft-spoken nyonya who seldom asserted herself, took a similar stand. She shocked him by kneeling down and wrapping her arms around his legs, "Gin Leng, don't go. I beg you, please. You are our only son. Stay alive please for us, for our sakes."

It felt as if his very heart was wrenched out of his skin as he looked out of the window and saw Jacq being dragged out by Japanese soldiers into a jeep, her clothes torn, kicking, scratching wildly, screaming agonising cries for help. The soldiers, followed by a collaborator hooded in white, jumped into the waiting jeeps, slammed the doors shut and drove away in a frenzy, leaving the terrified neighbourhood in stunned silence.

Only Gin Leng flailed and thrashed in his father's arms, howling like a trapped animal, utterly devastated. When they ran over to the Cordeiro house, they found the doctor and his son lying on the ground covered in blood, dead. In one swoop, Gin Leng had lost the kind elderly doctor friend he respected, his best friend Jacob, and the tomboy who lit up everyone's lives with her presence, the girl he was deeply in love with.

Gin Leng found himself in a state of limbo, waiting for the war to end, waiting for Jacq to come home. His parents feared he was going out of his mind. Every evening, he would walk over to Jacq's house and wait in the verandah, hoping Jacq would appear. Often, he locked himself in his room for hours, refusing to eat or talk to anyone, emerging with swollen red eyes.

Gin Leng's father, Baba Teoh, made inquiries through his network of contacts but no one knew where Jacq had been taken. They only heard the chilling news that the Japanese military was abducting young women to service their soldiers at 'comfort stations' set up in various parts of their conquered territories. He was certain Jacq must have been singled out as her beauty would not have gone unnoticed. He kept this information from his son, wanting to protect him from this ghastly news.

One stormy night, through sheets of pouring rain, Gin Leng saw an elderly Malay man on a bicycle at his front gate, drenched, looking lost.

"What do you want?" Gin Leng shouted above the howling wind.

"*Ini rumah* Gin Leng *ke?* This one Gin Leng house?"

"Ya, ya, *saya* Gin leng. It's me. *Apa lu mau?*"

Gin Leng grabbed an umbrella and ran out into the blinding rain.

The old man pulled out a small crumpled piece of paper tucked under his faded cotton sarong and pressed it into

Gin Leng's hands. His dull, watery eyes looked tired and devoid of life. He whispered despairingly to Gin Leng, "*Tolong, kesian dia, kesian dia orang semua.* Pity, very pity, help, *tolong.*"

Without another word, he got onto his bicycle and cycled away. Gin Leng, puzzled, walked back into the house and read the note. He could hardly believe what it implied.

> *Help me, help. I am being held prisoner at The House of Silken Flowers. In Hotel Tai Loke. In a row of shops across from Pudu jail. Get me out of here please... please. I cannot take this anymore. Jacq*

Baba Teoh used every contact he knew to help save Jacq after Gin Leng gave him the note. He contacted an ex-colleague, Hiroshi, a Japanese art teacher, a placid and spiritual man and tried to persuade him to 'patronise' Hotel Tai Loke to check out conditions for staging a rescue. Nyonya Eng Neo sold off her wedding jewellery to the pawnshop and pressing the money into Hiroshi's hands, the Teohs begged Hiroshi to buy time with Jacq at the brothel where she was imprisoned, to give her some respite from the ongoing assaults and plan her escape.

Hiroshi refused. He argued he did not want to jeopardise his position – it was too dangerous should the military find out he was spying on them. Furthermore, he refused to visit a brothel even if it were a rescue mission. But he offered a sliver of hope – he would write to a relative in Tokyo, a highly placed military officer and complain about this military set-up, specifically mentioning the House of Silken Flowers and report that a sixteen-year-old girl with European-Dutch parentage was being held there against her will.

Whether it was Hiroshi's letter or some other reason, no one knew. A few months later, the House of Silken Flowers was closed down suddenly. Gin Leng, spying on the place, noticed no activity around the shophouse anymore. The occupants had vanished completely. The building was all boarded up and barricaded with few traces left behind of its infamous glory apart from the dark, dingy cubicles upstairs, each with a bed inside, blocked off by cheap, flimsy curtains. Each cubicle had a small sign above its door with the name of a flower written in Japanese.

Fifty years later, when Gin Leng had given up hope of ever meeting Jacq, who would have thought he would find her again?

"It's Jacq, guys!" Gin Leng yelled, teetering unsteadily on his chair, pointing at the photo in the morning papers.

Over the last several years, the surviving members of the Fearless Five – Gin Leng, Siew Wai, Bertie and Nick made it a point to meet once every month. They were all in their sixties now, successful professionals with established careers and families of their own. Some of them had retired. Except for Bertie who had settled down in Singapore, all the rest lived in Kuala Lumpur and had more time to meet up now.

One Sunday, they were having breakfast at a coffee shop along Sultan Street in Chinatown. It was busy and noisy but the thick slices of bread grilled over a charcoal stove spread with delicious kaya and served with black coffee made it one of their favourite places for morning *yum cha*. Gin Leng was browsing through the morning papers when he chanced upon the article.

"She didn't die in the war! She's alive!"

They stared at Gin Leng, alarmed at his outburst. They knew of his undying, unspoken love for Jacq and how much he had suffered.

"Hey Gin, hallucinating or what?" asked Siew Wai in his usual direct manner.

"He's shaking and sweating. You alright, Gin?" Nick, now a renowned heart surgeon, questioned worriedly.

"Jacq, it's Jacq," gasped Gin Leng, "Look, she's in today's news!"

They grabbed hold of the newspapers and skimmed the article.

"Oh my God... it's her!" shouted Bertie.

"She survived! She survived it all and now she's fighting back!" gasped Siew Wai.

"This is unbelievable... where has she been all these years?" Nick uttered in amazement.

Gin Leng said, "I'm going to find her, guys. I told her I'd find her after the war."

"But the war ended a long time ago... she may be a totally changed person. It's obvious she doesn't want any contact with us... otherwise she would have..." Nick stopped when he saw the mixture of hope, joy and anguish on Gin Leng's face.

"I want to see her again," Gin Leng murmured softly.

His friends looked at Gin Leng. The expression on his face showed clearly there was no point in trying to dissuade him.

"You do what you've got to do, man," said Bertie gruffly, patting Gin Leng gently on his shoulder.

After persistent phone calls from Gin Leng, the journalist who wrote the article gave him a number to call. The stranger who answered provided an address in the neighbouring country of Indonesia.

He found himself outside a small stone cottage built during Dutch colonial times. It had taken him more than five hours to travel from Jakarta International Airport to this small village in the highlands of Central Java. The cottage was snugly hidden away from the main road behind thick verdant foliage. He got out of the car and paused outside, hesitant, unsure if it was wise to resurrect the past. He could hear familiar music from a piano wafting from the cottage, the lilting, melancholic notes of Beethoven's *Moonlight Sonata* and guessed he had found the right house.

His heart beat faster and faster as he approached the house. He noticed a wild lush garden filled with exotic green plants, ferns and palms. Not a single flower was to be seen in the garden, which Gin Leng found odd, as he remembered she loved flowers. The door was unlocked. He took off his shoes, knocked a few times. The ethereal, brooding notes of the *Moonlight Sonata* continued uninterrupted. Gently he pushed the door open.

In the front hall, he saw a woman seated at a piano, her back turned to him, lost in her music. She stopped, aware of a stranger's presence and swung around.

She jumped to her feet and stared at him for a while, then through the fog of memory and time, cried out, "Gin! It's you!"

Jacq looked paler and more fragile than he remembered. Something odd – a black patch covered her left eye. Her broad shoulders seemed slightly incongruous with her slight physique, her long wavy hair was cropped short, framing an enigmatic face. She wore a blue and white sarong and a simple white top. Gin Leng thought it was remarkable how despite all she had gone through and the years that had passed, she still possessed a dignified beauty about her.

"You've kept your promise, Gin," she muttered in dazed disbelief.

They stood there staring at each other, overwhelmed by memories and mixed feelings of sadness and joy. She gestured to him to take a seat across from her. His eyes followed her every movement, riveted by her presence, his love for her like quiet embers lodged deep within, glowing alive at the sight of her.

He yearned to reach out and hold her, to tell her he had never forgotten her, but he knew he had to be careful. He started haltingly, "When the war ended, I waited for you to return home, I waited every day, every year. But you never did. Everyone told me to give up, that you had probably been killed. I refused to believe them but eventually I gave up hope. Why did you not return, Jacq, or at least let me know you were alive?"

She replied calmly, only her voice betrayed her pain and anguish, "How could I? How could I go back to my previous life? I was a mess, a total abject mess. Damaged mentally, emotionally. I shunned men at all costs. I couldn't bear the sight and touch of them for a long time. I felt dirty and defiled, so ashamed. How could I meet you again? I had to disappear, go somewhere where no one knew me."

She smiled bitterly, "Ironic, isn't it? Considering I was part of an all-boys gang for the best years of my life... and my best friend was you."

She paused and looked at him gently.

"Do you have any children, Gin?" she asked.

"Oh," she added, "I should ask the more appropriate question first – are you married? And do you have children?"

Gin Leng tried to summarise, "Ten years after the war ended, I met someone, a girl called Lisa. We were married for thirty years. She's passed away. I have two children – they are all grown up now, the elder girl is married and has a two year old daughter. I'm a grandfather."

He wondered how she had survived all these years. She sensed his thoughts.

"After the war I drifted through several places and ended up here. Grandma Marguerite owned this house which she bequeathed to my mother. Aunt Dorothy, Mummy's sister, helped me a lot. I teach music here," she offered.

"I hope you don't mind me asking, but did you have an accident?" he asked, pointing to her eye patch.

It was then that she opened up and confided to him the horrors of the past, unable to keep them inside her any longer. Jacq looked down at her hands as she spoke very softly.

"A rape is enough to scar you a lifetime. Imagine what it's like to be raped every day and night? Thirty to forty men day and night. All of the girls were held there against their will. We were so young, just teenagers. There was a chubby little girl we called Baby, barely twelve years old. She didn't make it. We were all sorts - Chinese, Malays, Indians, Eurasians, East Indies, Filipino, it didn't really matter."

Jacq continued, "It was terrifying. The queue outside my room was endless, the soldiers coarse, rapacious. It was nothing I had ever imagined would happen to me. They named each of us after a flower. I was called Orchid. I can't bear flowers, not even the scent of them, to this day."

"I tried to make myself ugly. I cut off my hair, my

eyebrows in clumps. I smeared myself with faeces but was forced to eat it instead. I decided to mutilate myself – that would disgust them, I was sure. I stole the kitchen knife, heated it over a candle flame and pierced my left eye. I passed out from the pain. They revived me, beat me up severely and locked me in a tiny room for days. I was hauled back to my cubicle and the assaults started all over again. My blind eye didn't repel at all. I became a novelty instead – the girl with the green eye."

Gin Leng listened quietly at first, his fists clenched in anger. Tears streaming down his cheeks, he tried to find some sort of atonement.

"Forgive me Jacq, please forgive me. I did not come to your rescue... I heard your screams... but I didn't... I didn't run over to help you... I have been haunted by that all my life."

She responded flatly, "They were armed with guns, bayonets, knives. Daddy and Jacob tried to fight them. The Jap soldiers blasted their brains out in front of me. You did the right thing. I have never held that against you, Gin, you must know that."

She continued, "All I ever knew of physical love between man and woman was our farewell kiss up in the tree house that last moment we shared. After I was abducted, every single day was one of humiliation and sexual degradation.

"One girl named Ling went mad and they shot her. I realised had I blinded myself completely, they would have killed me too. I tried other ways to bear the suffering. My faith and my music kept me sane. Every night I prayed to God to save me, to end this torture. I played symphonies in my head, all that music swirling around me in the midst of brutal rape, Mozart, Beethoven, all the joyful melodies I could think of, my fingers running over imaginary ivory keys.

"It was impossible to escape with guards everywhere. The Mama-san in charge was cruel to the core, interested only in money. We begged the officers to help us but nothing worked. A few were sympathetic but refused to get involved. Only the old caretaker, Kassim was kind to us. He took a terrible risk delivering my message to you. They shut down the place suddenly a few months later. We were taken to a women's concentration camp – conditions were horrible, starvation, disease, death, but at least we were no longer sex slaves."

Gin Leng noticed her whole body was trembling. He said gently, "Please, Jacq, you don't need to go through all this again. Enough."

"I've not heard that name Jacq for such a long time. I miss it... I was so innocent then," she mused, her face lighting up briefly.

"For years I told no one. I kept it all inside, fearing I would be shunned if people knew the truth. I lead a very private life here. Then I read about the Korean comfort women demanding justice from the Japanese government. These women found the courage to come out in the open. I decided to come out too.

"Why should I hide away the rest of my life in shame?

I don't want money, I want retribution. I want a formal apology just like what the Korean women want. At the very least, I should be given a decent apology, atonement for the injustices I have suffered.

"I was only sixteen when I was taken. I am in my sixties now. It's time to do something. The world has got to know. That's what they'd like – no witnesses left to report this crime against humanity."

"I will do everything I can to help you, Jacq, if you'll allow me," Gin Leng offered.

It was on the tip of his tongue to ask her something important but would she think him a stupid romantic old fool? Surely it was too ridiculous a proposition. He had to fly home soon to Kuala Lumpur and he might not have a chance again. What if she disappeared again?

He watched Jacq as she leant back into her chair, spent and exhausted. She looked wan and on the edge, like a fragment of dainty rice paper just a crumple away, not the tomboy he adored who could arm wrestle lustily with the boys or slam a volleyball over the net with such power. A wisp of her wavy hair fell over her functioning eye. She brushed it aside and joked, "It's good for the neck muscles, you know, having one eye. You've got to swing your head around more."

He smiled, awed at her irrepressible spirit. He knelt down before her, "I still love you, Jacq."

She looked at him in astonishment, totally taken aback. He returned her gaze, deep into that one mesmerising darkish green eye.

"Does it not matter to you that I am a soiled, damaged woman?"

"You were a victim of war. All those acts were forced on you. They mean nothing to me. I love you, I always have. Now that I've found you I don't want to lose you. Do you think we could spend our lives together? I'd be deeply honoured if you say yes."

"It is very kind of you but it is too late. I am too far gone in life's journey. Too much baggage."

"Far gone? What does that mean? As long as we are alive, it's worth living. It is, Jacq, you must believe that, you must... especially with someone you love. Marry me Jacq. I've loved you for a lifetime and I still do."

"Well, I'll be damned. Let me think about it, Gin."

They spent the rest of the day talking and reminiscing about good times and old friends, steering away from painful topics like deadly land mines lurking just beneath the surface. Gin Leng noticed with some concern that she got tired and breathless easily. When he finally had to leave for Jakarta, she came to the door to say farewell. Touching his hand lightly, she said, "Thank you Gin."

"For what?"

"For everything. I've not been so happy... for a very long time," she smiled. The twinkle in her light green eye and the lightness in her step made him recall the way she used to be when she was young and carefree, a lifetime ago.

Gin Leng flew home to Kuala Lumpur on the last flight out of Jakarta.

Her words, "Let me think about it", gave him hope, something to hold on to. He wished he could call her every day to talk, to urge her to reach for happiness when it was within grasp. She had told him she would call once she'd made up her mind. Before that, she wanted to be left alone, to think it carefully through. He respected her decision. No pressure, no imposition of any kind at all on her.

A week after his trip to Jakarta, he still hadn't heard from her. He tested the phone on its handle every day to make sure it was working. Perhaps she had lost his phone number. Maybe she had written a letter instead and it got lost in the mail. What if she disappeared again? The stress was killing him. It had taken fifty years to find her again, what were a few more days? Just a few more days and she would surely call, and maybe... maybe, she would accept his proposal.

That morning, he browsed disinterestedly through the morning newspapers over a cup of coffee before heading to his office a short drive away. He paused all of a sudden. Was he going out of his mind? Jacq... it was Jacq again. There was a photo of Jacq in the papers! Only this time, the photo zoomed in on her face and the article, in just one short paragraph, had a heading:

Activist for plight of comfort women passes away
before trip to the UN

The article read,

> *Jacquelina Cordeiro, a renowned human rights*
> *activist fighting for the cause of the comfort women*
> *during World War II in Southeast Asia, was found*
> *dead in her home yesterday. Her body was discovered*
> *in the morning by her aunt who had dropped by for*
> *a visit. It is believed that the activist, in her sixties,*
> *had died of a heart attack. Her aunt has requested*
> *that no wreaths or flowers of any kind be sent to the*
> *home as Miss Cordeiro had an aversion to flowers.*
> *Miss Cordeiro was scheduled to make an appearance*
> *before the United Nations Commission of Human*
> *Rights next month to fight for compensation for*
> *Japan's World War II rape victims and to push for an*
> *official apology from the Japanese Government. Miss*
> *Cordeiro was unmarried and is survived by no known*
> *family members except her aunt to mourn her loss.*

Gin Leng staggered violently to his feet. The heavy
teak chair fell backwards on the floor with a loud crash.
Coffee splattered all over the newspapers, the dark blood-
like stain spreading out in a jagged, widening circle on the
cheap newsprint, smearing Jacq's tense, apprehensive face
in the photo.

He tore wildly at his shirt collar and the stifling tie around his neck, gasping, gulping for air. He couldn't breathe. Couldn't breathe at all.

His last words were, "Jacq, Jacq, it's her, Jacq."

*Gold embroidered Indonesian
nyonya slipper faces*

*Antique green kebaya with
orchid and fan motifs*

A Japanese tile featuring a Kilin, a mythological creature with the body of a lion

Silver key holder   *Silver belt buckle with two ladies on each side*

All images above courtesy Ken Yap

Moonlight Bay

Billy applies the brakes gently and nuzzles his car onto a patch of grass on one side of the road. It isn't well parked, its rear protrudes too far out on to the road, but then it really doesn't matter. Not any more. He steps out of the car, retrieves his bag from the boot, slams the door shut and crosses the road. Down a steep slope to one of his most loved places, Moonlight Bay, off the coast of Batu Ferringhi.

This secluded bay must have been named by an incurable romantic, he muses, even in his darkest of moods. It is enchanting in the moonlight. He himself fell under its spell when he was nineteen, strolling on the beach here with Isabelle for the first time. The moon shone like a giant South Sea pearl in the darkening sky, wreathed by wispy cloud ribbons. Was it the moon that evening that caused him to lose his senses? Or was it his love for the girl of his dreams, Isabelle, she who had captured his heart the moment he first saw her and loved ever since?

Impulsive as always, she had suddenly stopped in her tracks as they walked hand in hand on the beach and exclaimed, "Oh look! Look at the stars above! Hundreds of them. Where's Orion?"

How can a boy resist the temptation when this lovely girl looks up straining for a glimpse of her favourite constellation, all wide-eyed and excited, searching the starry sky. She was irresistible. He pulled her close to him. She was softness and curves and fitted comfortably into his arms. He bent gently over her, his lips searching for hers. He heard her murmur surprise, then a soft sigh. He tasted her lips, her mouth, felt an electric charge running though him. After that first kiss, they strolled in silence, not wanting to spoil the magic with the uselessness of words. The sea was calm that night, an indigo blanket softened by a shimmering path to the moon. That seems like eons ago now.

He clambers down the last stretch of the slope, takes off his sandals, enjoys the feel of the soft powdery sand under his feet. A dazzling sky-blue, the sea is tranquil this early Sunday morning. Waves break serenely in white lacy ripples on the sand. At his usual picnic spot, he takes off his shorts and shirt worn over his swimming togs, puts them in the bag, places it and his sandals under the shady umbrella tree. Doggedly, he wades into the sea towards a huge boulder on the left side of the bay. It is not high tide yet but he has to swim out a bit to get to the boulder. Its sides are slippery, encrusted with barnacles; he is obsessed with getting on top of it. After a few painful cuts on his feet, he manages to clamber on. He lies down on the massive rock, enjoying the warm rays of the morning sun. The sea makes gurgling, gloopy sounds as the waves gently hit against the boulder.

Tears stream down his face even as he tries to blink away the salt water and the glaring sun.

How to get rid of this terrible aching pain? This heartbreak devouring him? How to let go and what was that, 'move on'? She had left him. The love of his life, Isabelle, had left him, just like that. When they both went overseas to further their studies in two different countries, he to Australia, she to the UK, they worried it would be the end of their relationship, their Form Six romance. She asked him to stay faithful to her and he had. No one could match up to her, nor ever take her place, he knew. He asked her to mix around, to feel free, so that she would be really sure she wanted to be with him after her studies abroad. When they both returned to Penang after graduation, they were deeply in love with each other still. They found good jobs and the courtship resumed. He proposed to her right here on this boulder at Moonlight Bay, their secret rendezvous place.

He remembers how beautiful she looked as the sun shone on her shoulders that morning. They had come out here for an early morning swim. He hadn't planned to propose that morning, but looking at her, splashing water, throwing her head back in laughter as he returned her splashes, kicking her tanned legs in the air, one strap of her turquoise swimming costume falling over her shoulder, he blurted out, "I want you to be the mother of my children!"

"What?" she looked at him, taken by surprise.

She burst out laughing, "Are you proposing to me here? You idiot," she teased, "Whatever happened to moonlight and roses? Can't you wait for a moonlit night or somewhere dark and romantic?"

Before he could reply, she giggled, "Oh wait, I'm being presumptuous. Was that a marriage proposal or are you just asking me to have children with you?"

She didn't need any clarification from him. She could see in his eyes how much he loved and adored her, how proud and happy he would be if she would be his wife.

"I accept. It's yes to both," she replied in her cheeky playful way, splashing him again. He remembers jumping up to his feet whooping with joy, then diving into the water. He swam underwater for quite a distance in sheer bliss, unrestrained, unfettered, his heart soaring with happiness. When his lungs felt like bursting, he swam back to the boulder, popping up near where her legs were. She screamed at him, fear in her eyes.

"Don't ever do that again, you horrid man! I thought you'd drowned!"

Then, a month ago, on a Friday evening, he returned home to a strangely empty house and found a note from her on her dressing table. A Dear-John sort of letter, thank you for the good times but I am in love with someone else and please forgive me bla-bla-bla sort of letter. It was hard to believe something like this could happen. He tried to call her but there was no reply. He went to her office but they said she had gone on long leave. He searched for her in all the familiar places, even here at Moonlight Bay, but she had disappeared.

Everything looked surreal without her. Her pink toothbrush sitting in her mug with the words 'Be X-traordinary' mocked him every morning. The black high heels she wore on their last dinner outing were still in the foyer, one standing, the other lying nonchalantly on its side. All the things she loved – her potted plants, the stone *apsara* from Angkor, painted lacquer boxes from a trip to the Taj Mahal, a celadon vase from her best friend, her cassette discs and books – hogged the same places. Her pillow still smelt of her. What had possessed her to leave all these precious objects behind? After all they had gone through, the lonely years of separation and the love they shared for each other, was he so dispensable – to be dropped off like dirty laundry at the dry cleaners?

Yesterday, on Christmas day, he had turned down all invitations to parties and gatherings. He was not in the mood for revelry. In fact, he found himself wanting to whack anybody who dared to smile, an agonising desire to punch anyone who laughed. His mother dropped by to check on him, concerned he was not looking after himself, locking himself away from the rest of the world. She cooked his favourite dish, her delicious, spicy Penang prawn mee topped with mint leaves, and brought it over in a *tengkat*, a three tiered container, for his lunch. He had no appetite for it nor anything else; he had not eaten for days. She was worried at his listlessness and bitterness, his loss of interest in life.

"Son, you can only grieve so much, then you've got to move on," she advised.

"You wouldn't understand what I'm going through, Ma," he mumbled.

"You may feel that life is not worth living right now, but believe me, it will get better," she said, putting her hand gently on his shoulder.

He did not answer his mother, just sat there, incommunicado and morose.

She looked at him sadly and sighed, "I wish something could happen, something that can shake you out of this despondency. Please Billy, snap out of it, enough of this self-pity."

She picked up her car keys and left to attend a Christmas cantata, giving him a hug first. Her own husband left her when Billy was just a baby; she had refused to tell him anything about his father. It was Ji Eee, his second aunt who told him his *see lang* father had run off with a shampoo girl from the Ayer Itam barber shop. Ji Eee always referred to his father as *see lang,* which means dead person in Penang Hokkien, to show her disgust but had no idea whether he was dead or still alive. He wondered where his mother found the inner strength but maybe she didn't love his Dad enough, not the way he loved Isabelle.

So, when Billy drove out here early this morning to

Moonlight Bay, where it had all started – his first kiss, the place where he'd proposed to Isabelle, it was to purge himself of her. This burden of shock, heartbreak and betrayal was too hard to bear. He loved the sea. It must be liberating to just swim on and on to the unreachable horizon, disappear into the watery depths. When Isabelle learns he has vanished at Moonlight Bay, she would have to carry this retribution for the rest of her life. How can you let a man love you in his every breath and pore, love you beyond comprehension and then just up and leave? How could you, Isabelle?

He realises he has forgotten to take off his watch. It is a first wedding anniversary present from Isabelle. They've been married for only a year, he can't recall saying or doing anything that might have hurt her feelings. In her Dear-John letter, she made it clear it wasn't his fault. She had run away with his best friend, someone from his childhood days, his best man at their wedding. One betrayal was hard, but this double betrayal left him spent, wasted. This would be his goodbye letter, no need for words, his bag with his watch, belongings and sandals left behind at Moonlight Bay would say it all. She would get the message.

He swims back to shore, takes off his watch and puts it into his bag. It is the usual crowd on a pleasant Sunday morning. A family is picnicking under the shady trees. The little child dozes on an inflatable mattress while her family members sit on a mat eating with their fingers, small containers of food spread around them. Some teenagers are happily playing Frisbee, while others are swimming or playing in the waves. A father in a pair of shorts with red hibiscus patterns watches protectively over his children building a sandcastle. Crouched under a spindly green polka-dotted umbrella, is the mother, obviously no sun lover, covered in long sleeves, long pants, sunglasses, a wide-brimmed hat. A Japanese couple is busy taking photographs, the fair-skinned Japanese lady making V signs for every pose. Two pale, lanky blondes in bikinis lie tummy down, sunbathing on towels, possibly just arrived from a wintry Europe. In the distance, a cluster of locals are busy digging for *siput*, snails, in the sand. A scene of happy, idyllic contentment and he is the only raging, depressed misfit.

He walks resolutely down the sloping beach towards the sea. The sea recedes before him. How peculiar. Every step he takes, the sea recedes further. This is totally unexpected. Tides do not go out this quickly. He has been visiting Moonlight Bay since childhood, is familiar with its moods and tidal patterns. He has never seen anything like this before. In a matter of minutes, the sea has disappeared! In front of him stretches a barren sea bed with swathes of mud and rocks, as if someone has pulled out a plug from the ocean floor. He is astonished to see tiny flashes of silver on the bedrock – fishes flapping, writhing, stranded by the tide.

The air has become deathly still. The birds have all strangely disappeared even though the sky remains bright and sunny. The pair of patchy-brown mongrels lazing on the sand earlier have skulked away, tails between their legs. An air of heavy expectation is building up. He can't figure out what it is. People are walking nearer and nearer to the edge of the shore, curious, puzzled over the strange phenomenon. Some children and adults clutching toy buckets run joyfully out to collect the fish.

He strains his eyes out to the horizon. Far out at sea, a dazzling white horizontal line stretches right across the bay. An astonishing armada of magnificent white stallions, manes flying wildly, plumes creating a misty spray, is advancing at an incredible speed, frothing, seething. As it comes closer, everyone is rooted to the spot, spellbound by the ominous wall of water building up beneath the foaming, raging crests. A roar of a million thundering hooves fill the bay.

"Tsunami! Tsunami! Run! Run! Tsunami coming!" yells out someone.

Billy swings around, notices it is the Japanese man taking photos earlier. He is jumping up and down frantically, gesticulating wildly, gone stark raving mad.

"Tsunami! Run, run! Tsunami!" both he and now his girlfriend too, are screaming at everyone on the beach.

The response is one of puzzlement and disbelief. People react sluggishly at first. Like a slow motion picture, some folks reluctantly begin rolling up their mats and towels or grudgingly pack up their picnic things. Some sceptics refuse to budge and sit down to watch more action unfold. Others run out even further, trying to figure out the strange phenomenon. As it approaches nearer and nearer, it becomes apparent this is a colossal wave racing forwards. The advancing wall of water is now almost twenty feet tall, turning a transparent yellowish-green at the top beneath the fizzing, foaming crest. Pandemonium breaks out as it dawns on all this is a deadly killer wave. Parents shriek at their children busy catching fish to turn around and run. Everyone begins to run in all directions. The bay resounds with screams and howls of terror.

Billy dashes swiftly back towards the boulder he rested on earlier. He knows if he clambers over the pile of rocks and boulders, he will reach the promontory and scale up the cliff there. He has done it before – on a challenge during a boy scout camping trip here at midnight. He scrambles over the rocks with the skill of a mountain goat he didn't know he possessed. The huge monster wave is almost upon them now. As the gargantuan wave hits, he grabs a branch of the tree overhanging on the cliff and clings on to it for dear life.

The wave hits with a tremendous force, attacking everything with unimaginable fury. He feels as if the entire Indian Ocean has emptied itself here, the water engulfs him, thrashing, churning. The angry sea slaps and pummels in seething, raging violence. Branches snap all around him. Wreckage spins mercilessly, the sea a giant washing machine gone berserk. His grip on the branch slips a little, he is running out of breath, cannot hold on much longer.

The raging, rushing waters recede suddenly. The sea begins to ebb, sucked out by a mighty force. Billy splutters and gasps for breath, limp, exhausted. He doesn't have a moment to lose – he has to climb higher. A tsunami isn't solitary, it strikes in clusters, he recalls from a Form Five physical geography class. Frantically, he scrambles up the branches of the tree. His body and limbs feel like they've gone through a shredder, torn and bleeding. He climbs up and up in a desperate frenzy till he reaches a tree trunk protruding out of the vertical cliff. A mighty roar rumbles throughout the bay as the second wave approaches – bigger, higher, a moving mountain of terrifying, blue-green water with an energy and force that surpasses an atom bomb.

Nothing, he is sure, nothing can survive this. No more time to climb and no strength left in him. Wrapping himself tightly around the tree trunk, he says a silent goodbye. It is his mother he thinks of as he faces death, not Isabelle. His mother who has loved him unconditionally, who he knows will love him always. He needs a lifetime to make up for the way he's behaved, to atone for his supercilious attitude. He doesn't want to go, not yet, please God not yet, forgive me for thinking of dying, please, please God I don't want to die, I don't want to die....

When the second wave hits, it finishes off everything the first wave has not destroyed, crashing onto the main road with a mighty roar, washing away cars and buses, uprooting houses, snapping up trees, fishing boats, telephone and power lines like toothpicks. It dumps a 30-foot yacht on the road. The earth groans and rumbles at this cataclysmic disaster. Billy clings on to the narrow tree trunk, locked in a vice-like grip, witnessing what looks like the end of the world. The trunk shudders but does not break. Perched high above the bay, it is spared the onslaught of the mighty waves.

When the waves have subsided and the sea has calmed down, Billy climbs wearily, slowly down to the bay, bloodied and limping. It is a scene of total devastation. A once entrancing bay of startlingly blue water is now a wasteland of rubble, debris and mud. He trips over something and is shocked to find it is a dead body. He staggers backwards in fright; he has never encountered death before. The contrast is too awful to bear; the idyllic scene this morning and now the horror, the horror of it all. He trips again over another object on the muddy floor and falls flat on the ground. A pale, disembodied child's face buried in the slimy mud stares up at him, eyes wide open, just inches away. He gapes at the lifeless eyes in horror and revulsion. He flounders in the mud, struggling to get up on wobbling legs, his hands clutching his stomach desperately to stop himself from retching.

Weeping, Billy tries to conjure up the face of the woman he loves but he can't remember how she looks. He struggles to visualise Isabelle's face, her lips, her expressive eyes. His mind is blank. Slowly, he gets up on his feet and limps towards the road. Isabelle's gone for good. The 'something' his mother referred to may not have been what she had in mind, but it has done the trick. Life is more important than love.

Beaded tablecloth with sea blue background
(Image courtesy the Peranakan Museum, Singapore)

I spent much of my growing-up years by the sea. On the left is my mother, my elder sister Su Win and me at Port Dickson. On the right, a photo of our faithful amah carrying me with my mother and sister. Both photos were taken by my father.

Motifs of sea creatures are quite popular with the babas and nyonyas. The top row shows two examples of kebaya sulam with motifs of sea animals. Below, the left image shows a kebaya renda (lace kebaya) with motifs of shrimps, which are symbols of happiness, good fortune and longevity. (Image courtesy Ken Yap) The right image shows a kebaya renda belonging to the author with motifs of fish – symbols of wealth in abundance.

A Light Bulb Moment

Ah Ma ah, my boyfriend ask me to marry him leh. Larsnite he proposed.

Chann keh? Really ah? Wah so fast, walk together short while wan to marry oredi! Sure or not?

Ya lor... I don't mind wor. I like him a lot. He very unusual.

You oredi thirty years old... very soon nobody wan. Okay lah okay lah better quickly say yes.

Aiya I'm not that desperate, I'm marrying for love lah.

Why he so funny wan ah? You sure he Chinese boy meh? Maybe he bluffing... maybe he Muslim? Aiyo die lor cannot eat pork.

No lah Ah Ma. He is Chinese. Got Chinese surname what. His mother even more Chinese than you... pray to this Chinese god, that Chinese god, Buddha, emperor god, always pai sun one.

Then why he cannot speak Chinese? And why so dark colour one his skin?

Aiyahhh Ah Ma, millions of Chinese all over the world... not all the same mah but these baba Chinese why like that I oso not sure...

Baba? What is that? I oni know Baa baa black sheep...

Donald say the men are called baba, the women nyonya. I don't know much, okay? Now oni learning a bit. Their names are Chinese, sometimes they oso got old-fashioned English *names. He say they follow Chinese customs but then his mother ah, wear sarong, eat with fingers and speak Baba Malay. All campur campur oredi.*

So funny one huh... I deen know wor. Myself Cantonese, come from Jinjang New Village. When I married your father, oredi confusing becos he Hailam.

Aiyoh sei lor, I'm late oredi. Got to go or else stuck in traffic jam. Bye bye, fai tik chou ler.

Ei ei, daughter, wait! When getting married? Got set day oredi?

That conversation took place between my mother and I five years ago. She was always going on about my ticking biological clock so naturally, she was overjoyed when I told her I was getting hitched. Who would have thought my marriage would become such a mess after five years?

When I met Donald, I was already thirty years old and still single. He was tall and dark, a bit on the plump side and I found his swarthy good looks attractive. I was thrilled when he proposed marriage after a brief courtship though I did wonder why he had been a bachelor for forty years. It wasn't my business, really, perhaps he never found the right person. I was in love and found him charming, courteous and kind. Extroverted by nature, a party animal, I was the carefree, happy-go-lucky type. Much has changed since. I am often nervous, easily agitated and suffer from anxiety attacks. Unlike my gregarious character in the past, I have become a semi-recluse, preferring to hide in my bedroom when I'm at home. Friends have noticed this drastic change in my character. How can marriage change one so? Well, it certainly wasn't the wrong choice of husband, it was the other woman. It was his mother!

From the start, Donald and I wanted a simple, quiet wedding. We didn't have much money and couldn't afford the showy format many young couples opted for in sumptuous hotel ballroom settings with a live band and powerpoint ad nauseum of the couple's baby photos right through courtship to the wedding day. We couldn't afford to dash to a beach in Bali, take videos of us running slow-motion into each other's arms or looking dreamily into each other's eyes, in an array of wedding gowns and traditional costumes. All we could pay for was a simple wedding dinner for family members and some close friends.

My future mother-in-law's domineering, intrusive character began to emerge, to my chagrin. As Donald and I discussed our wedding plans, she plonked herself down between us and mouth puckering in scorn, she whined, "*Amboii*, why so small scale? *Malu sia*! Cannot like this! Lose face only! Donald is my only son. We must have a big grand wedding! I want to invite all my relatives, friends, neighbours and previous neighbours. We must have fifty tables at least and nothing less than a six-star hotel."

I was flabbergasted. At ten guests per table Chinese wedding dinner-banquet style, this would mean a total of 500 guests and an astronomical amount of money. I dug in, "No *lah*, Donald and I have discussed this. We want a small, cosy wedding, not a flashy extravaganza where we don't know anybody."

She glared at me looking terribly insulted, then turned towards Donald, her eyes brimming with tears, "My son, you cannot deny your mother this one and only chance. I've waited all my life for this. Your poor father died young but I know he will agree up there in heaven you cannot marry like a common beggar! Cannot, cannot!"

"Er... erhhm... ya, Mak, I see your point but... er... you see, Sau Ping and I have just put down a large sum of money as deposit for a house, we don't have... er... much money to splash around."

"A house?" she queried, bewildered, as if she'd never heard of it before. "House? Who cares about a house? A wedding is once in a lifetime. It's got to be spectacular!" she insisted.

I kept silent, gritting my teeth, willing Donald to stay firm.

She dabbed at her tears with a handkerchief looking suitably dejected, playing the role of now-I'm-old-nobody-cares-to-listen to perfection, her alert eyes downcast, darting from side to side.

Then, in a tone of great sacrifice, she announced,

"I give up. Young people are so rebellious nowadays. Okay *lah*! A small, miserable wedding then. No need fifty tables, just thirty-eight will do. 38 is a good number. Anything less I'm not going to show my face, *malu sia*," she offered her so-called compromise.

Donald acquiesced, nodding obediently, to my utter dismay.

In the end, Donald and I had to pay for the entire wedding. Not only did we have to pay for the exorbitant hotel wedding costs, clothes, food, wine, photography, flowers, we also had to pay for hotel accommodation for all her relatives from out of town.

"This is crazy. Why can't they pay for their own accommodation?" I asked her pointedly.

"Ah *lah*... Sau Ping, people coming all the way to Kuala Lumpur for your wedding... they've got nowhere to stay... you have to provide accommodation what... and our place is so small, no space, *malu sia*."

"If they can't pay, then don't come *lah*!" I muttered under my breath.

"What's wrong with your mother?" I grumbled to Donald in private, "always *malu sia*, *malu sia*... everything is shameful to her. Everything must show off, must be big and grand!"

"Where else but at a wedding to flaunt your wealth?"

Donald answered.

"It's okay if you have tons of money but we don't!"

Donald told me in confidence his mother had inherited a substantial amount of money from her late parents. He assumed she would help to subsidise the colossal cost of the wedding expenses. It turned out that my mother-in-law refused to fork out a single sen to help defray costs. The wedding ang pows she insisted would repay the wedding bills did not materialise. My uncles and aunts, even though they came from working class backgrounds, were exceedingly generous in their angpows. It was her stingy relatives who were annoyingly inconsiderate, bringing their entire family along with four children in tow and the kitchen sink, gifting us with miserly ang pows as if they were gold bullion. We started our marriage 50,000 ringgit in debt. Our plans for a short honeymoon at the nearest hill station, Fraser's Hill, had to be aborted. Just as well, I thought, for she would have insisted on coming along.

Earlier on, Donald had asked me if I would mind living in the same house with his widowed mother when he proposed marriage. He could not let her live by herself, he explained. I agreed without any reservations. I got along very well with senior folks and didn't think it would be a problem. After all, it was my grandma who took care of me when my mother had to help out at our grocery shop in Klang. A grandparent at home would be a boon to a young family, I thought, an extra pair of eyes to watch over the children when they arrived.

We moved into our new home, a small terrace house in the suburbs a few months after the wedding. It had a basic design of a lounge, dining room, utility room and kitchen downstairs, three bedrooms upstairs and a tiny pocket handkerchief lawn – the usual unimaginative layout for the lower middle-income category. Both Donald and I were overjoyed at owning a house of our own, even though it came with a heavy mortgage. MIL, what I called my mother-in-law, delayed us by refusing to move from Donald's rented flat until an auspicious date chosen by geomancers and prayers at the temple.

On the day we moved in, I noticed nine old cupboards belonging to MIL arriving in two truckloads. The enormous cupboards filled up her own bedroom upstairs, the tiny staircase landing, the spare room downstairs, the narrow corridor leading to the kitchen and spilled into the main lounge. I tried to protest but it was non-negotiable – the cupboards had been gifts on her wedding day and would stay with her till the day she died.

To make matters worse, she was a hoarder – duplicates and triplicates of everything from woks, *belangahs*, frying pans, pots, kettles, clocks, a massive collection of mismatched cutlery, plates, cups, ladles, mugs and serving dishes. Her kitchen things took up all the space in my kitchen, leaving me with only half of a cabinet. She boasted to relatives on the phone that her son had bought her a fabulous brand new house which sounded more and more like a gargantuan bungalow rather than a link house in a nondescript housing estate. I felt helpless, more like a tenant than the owner as her entire life's possessions filled up all the space.

It was hard starting out marital life drowning in debt but we managed to gradually settle our debts by taking on extra jobs. I joined a direct-selling pyramid scheme peddling health supplements beside holding a fulltime job while Donald worked long hours as a factory supervisor. I could live with the debts incurred. I could even live with her cumbersome cupboards. It was the day-to-day living with my mother-in-law, her sarcastic innuendos and her constant, lurking presence that drove me nuts.

MIL was everywhere, watching my every move, always trying to anticipate my actions so she could pre-empt me. She'd rush to the kitchen and hover when I tried to cook, grabbing everything I used, restoring it to its original position as if they were diamond-studded. The plastic bottle of sugar, the leaky bottle of soya sauce, the chipped enamel jar of cheap salt, the gigantic bottle of cooking oil bought at basement bargain price from the hypermarket – she would pick up every item after me, lips twitching curses, facial features frozen into perennial offendedness.

Her thin eyebrows would shoot up in horror when I walked to the fridge and pulled out a packet of chicken wings from the freezer or helped myself to some eggs. When I casually picked up some garlic pips or shallots from the plastic red basket, she'd go ballistic, rushing to count the remainder, grumbling that there weren't enough left to cook her curry *tumis* for the evening. Soon I stopped cooking altogether, unable to bear her unpleasant presence in the kitchen.

I was the competitor for her son's affection and attention, I realised. He was the sun, the moon, everything to her. Every morning, she got up very early, tidied the house, prepared breakfast for him and a packed lunch to take to work. Every evening, he returned home to a piping hot, home-cooked meal of six of his favourite dishes plus *kueh* for dessert. She told me to stay away from "her kitchen" as her son could not bear my bland, boring food.

When Donald came home from work, she would rush to open the front door for him the moment she heard his car coming up the driveway. Every time he drank a glass of water, she'd pick up his empty glass and wash it for him. She walked blithely into our master bedroom to pick up his dirty laundry. I couldn't believe my eyes when she went into the toilet to flush after him! If he had to work till late, she would wait, heat up his dinner, watch him eat then wash up after him. I wondered why my husband even needed a wife! When we went out together, she walked hand in hand with him, clutching him tightly in case she tripped. I soldiered on behind, carrying her ten-kilo handbag as the dutiful daughter-in-law.

MIL made it clear to me from the beginning how disappointed she was her beloved son had married "below" him. She pretended to be sweet and compliant with Donald around, but showed her true colours in his absence. One evening, she sighed loudly and sorrowfully as she ironed Donald's shirts, "*Kesian* that poor Betsy, such a nice girl, pity only. Donald really liked her."

"Who's Betsy?" I fell for her bait.

"Aiyee, you don"t know who's Betsy? Donald didn't tell you?"

"No, he didn't. Who is she?"

"Everybody thought Donald would marry her, the whole of Malacca and Singapore also know about their romance. She's his second cousin, really nice girl, so well brought up from a very rich family. She and Donald were playmates when they were young. And she's very beautiful. Not like..."

She hesitated, a very pregnant pause, her eyes travelled my stout figure, shabby T-shirt with an armpit tear and "No Money No Honey" slogan and feet in Hello Kitty towel slippers. She rolled her eyes in despair.

I kept quiet.

She continued, "And what's more, she's a teacher! Nothing like marrying a teacher, the best job in the world. For a woman. Half day only."

"But see *lah* my son, go and marry a woman who's not

highly educated, no degree, what kind of job... *apa lu mia kerja?* Admin assistant? What is that?"

I should have retreated to my bedroom, away from her sarcastic comments.

As she ironed her son's pyjamas next, she continued dolefully, "Somemore, Betsy is a nyonya... a true blue nyonya. From such a good high-class family. Of all people Donald go and marry a Hailam girl."

I was about to explode, "Just what the fuck is wrong with marrying a Hailam?"

Donald's noisy old Mitsubishi drove up the driveway. She dropped her iron in a hurry, tugged her sarong tightly around her waist, and rushed to the door to welcome her beloved home.

"You finish your apple already?" she asked, trailing me like a bad conscience.

" Huh? What apple?"

"There the apple you ate halfway this morning and put inside my fridge."

"Oh? Oh ya the apple! I had to rush to work, didn't have time to finish. I kept it in the fridge, didn't want to waste."

"Yes I know... I can see it there. The whole day long. You finish it already?"

"Okay, okay I'm going to eat it now," I marched to the

kitchen to gulp it down. Couldn't have it taking up all the space in her precious fridge, could I?

She muttered, loud enough for me to hear, "Apple already turn black..."

Every time I picked up a spoon to make a cup of coffee, she'd watch with eagle eyes and question, "Finish your coffee?"

"Huh no... why?"

"Nothing." A few minutes later, "Finish your coffee?"

Once I gulped down the last dregs, she would yank out her precious teaspoon, wash it vigorously then put it back in its assigned space.

Her possessiveness over everything from her son down to the frayed coconut husk doormat grated on my nerves. Having to put up with her barbed innuendos affected my self-esteem and my once relaxed state of mind. This constant scrutiny was harmless yet irritatingly harmful, like having to listen to someone scratching her fingernails across a chalkboard. All the time.

When I gave birth to a baby girl in the second year of my marriage, she kept harping that the family line was doomed. She refused to carry nor even look at her granddaughter for the first few months until she was won over by the cute baby girl. After that, MIL swung to the other extreme, fussing over the grandchild, dictating to me how to take care and bring up my own daughter. I resented it deeply. My friends who shared fun times eating, drinking and karaoke-ing at my place during my bachelor girl days, now stayed away because

MIL told them her weak heart and blood pressure could not handle any noise. For years I tried my best to keep the peace with MIL, keeping silent, being respectful, absorbing all the hurts, retreating into the peace and quiet of my bedroom.

One beautiful Sunday morning, my pent up feelings erupted. My daughter Suzanna was turning five. On an impulse, I felt like baking cupcakes for her birthday. I had never baked anything for my daughter, in fact, I had never baked at all since getting married. Just as I feared, the noise from the cake beater brought MIL into the kitchen. She looked at my polka dot apron, the ingredients spread out on the table, the baking tray with bright floral paper cups arranged neatly. Gritting her teeth and grumbling, she started rearranging things, examining the sugar in the bottle, wiping the smudges of flour and milk spills, washing the cutlery and crockery when I hadn't even finished yet. She grabbed the kettle to boil water to get rid of the grease. My blood began to boil too.

I jumped when she barked,

"Why you use my *bawang putih*? My garlic is all gone!"

"What? I didn't use any garlic! I'm not even cooking. I'm baking!"

"No more garlic! How come there's no more garlic? Who took my garlic?"

I ignored her.

"Why you use my spoon?" she persisted.

I was born under the Taurus zodiac sign and like a bull prodded far too many times, I finally snapped.

As she scrubbed her precious little teaspoon, I flung open the door of one of "her cabinets", reached for her favourite casserole dish – the one with the English roses pattern – and smashed it on the floor. Then I dumped my entire buttery cake mixture into the trash bin, switched off the oven and stomped upstairs to my room, tears of fury blurring my vision.

"You *gila perempuan*! *Perempuan hantu*! Mad woman! Devil!" I could hear her shrieking.

She wouldn't speak to me for days after that. The silence was simply blissful.

Matters reached a crisis point shortly after and triggered what I call the lightbulb moment. That night, I didn't realise our little daughter Suzanna was playing with her dolls behind our bed. I was lying in bed chatting with my husband, away from the prying ears of my mother-in-law. The bed creaked and groaned under Donald's enormous weight. The spring mattress wasn't springy anymore, depressing itself into a mini caldera where he positioned himself before lying down.

I sighed exasperatedly. I was tired of nagging Donald to stop eating such a huge quantity of food at dinnertime as he was severely overweight. My mother-in-law always cooked impressive but calorie-loaded meals for Donald.

Tonight he had gorged on *sotong sambal*, prawn and pineapple curry, pig trotters in vinegar, fried chicken and more. A nyonya cook, I have observed, is only satisfied when her target audience has taken a second or third helping. The moment his plate was almost empty, she would pile more and more food onto his plate.

The doctors had warned Donald to lose weight urgently. My nagging fell on deaf ears as he loved to eat and enjoyed his mother's food far too much. I decided to ditch the nagging and get to grips with reality.

"Donald, as you insist on eating yourself to an early death, I hope you've put my name down as beneficiary in your life insurance policy. Have you done it or not?"

My gentle, amiable husband as usual responded mildly. It was always hard to get him worked up over anything. "Don't be silly *lah*. What makes you so sure you'll outlive me?"

"Well, that's pretty obvious! You have high blood pressure, high cholesterol, diabetes, gout and you are twenty-five kilos overweight. You have all the problems of rich people who eat rich. Only in your case, you got no money. Doubly unfair *leh*."

"Better to live and die young, than die old and never live," he joked good-naturedly, plucking a quote from some cheesy Hollywood movie or mindless Whatsapp meme.

"Precisely. If you insist on dying young, don't you think it's a good idea Suzanna and I continue to, as you say, 'live'?"

"Er... actually come to think of it... I think it's still in my mother's name. When I first started work, I put her name down as beneficiary. I haven't updated it."

"Donald, die *lah*, how can? Can go and change it or not? The way things are between your mother and me, she's not going to give me a sen! And let's face it, it is your mother who is killing you off slowly, surely, day by day."

Ummppfffhh... zzzzz... snort.... zzzzzz

He was dead to the world, snoring like a cranky bad-tempered motorboat before a more sonorous rhythm set in.

I noticed Suzanna's foot sticking out from behind the base of my bed.

"Suzanna! What are you doing here? Time to go to bed."

I read her a bedtime story of a wicked ugly witch fattening two children lost in the woods for a gastronomic experience. After my daughter fell asleep, I went back to my room which now sounded like a showroom with a quadrophonic sound system. Even the water in my Ikea glass on the bedside table trembled, Jurassic Park-style, every time Donald's snoring reached a crescendo.

I could hardly sleep. Every few minutes, Donald's regular snoring switched to rasping gargles and throttled chokes. I slapped his enormous shaking tummy, growling a "Shatup!" He stopped snoring briefly, then the orchestra would strike up again. The next morning, I stumbled zombie-like downstairs, headed to the kitchen for a desperately needed coffee before driving to work.

MIL stormed into the kitchen waving a feather duster with a shock of red cockerel feathers, raging at me, "You *celaka perempuan*! Why you say I kill my son?"

"What? Who told you that?"

"My granddaughter! She said you said I am killing her Daddy. You *gila*? You mad ah? Why you say me like that?"

I turned cold, aghast at how my words were misinterpreted. I did not have the time nor the energy to explain, nor was she in the mood to listen.

"You know what? It's a small matter. Miscommunication. I'm late for work. I don't want to discuss this. I'll explain when I come home tonight."

"Oh now you so *pandai*... very clever izzit don't want to discuss... everything must discuss... cannot talk ah... your office very important, I not important... you *pakai baju* go to office while I do all the donkey work... cook, wash, bring up your children... you low class woman... *bangun pagi ta'da lipat selimut*... go to work come back... that's all you do... I am your maid... you *kurang ajar*."

She screamed at me as I walked out to my car. "Why you say I want to kill my son? Why you don't like me?"

"I just don't like you!" I shouted back.

I jumped into my car, zoomed down the driveway and sped off, almost crashing into an oncoming truck.

I returned home very late that night, caught in a snarling jam because of a heavy thunderstorm. Donald was already home as his car was parked in the porch. Exhausted and hungry, I went to the kitchen to find some dinner. When I switched on the light, a loud popping sound burst out and glass shattered onto the floor. The light bulb had blown. Wearily, I went to the storeroom and returned with a new bulb and a ladder.

"What's up, dear? Why is it so dark here?" Donald came downstairs to check.

"The light bulb blew. Careful, there are glass shards all over. I'll replace it with a new one."

"Here, let me do it," he offered.

Before I could stop him, he had his foot on the ladder and was climbing up. The ladder squeaked and groaned as he climbed higher and began to wobble. I grabbed hold of the ladder and muttered, "Donald, this is a bad idea. You're too heavy, better come down!"

"Nah, it'll be okay... pass me the bulb, please."

As I reached up to pass it to him, MIL's piercing screams filled the darkened kitchen, "AIIIYYYEEEE... You mad woman! It's you! You are the one killing my son! Murderer! Get down, Donald, get down!"

Both Donald and I were startled out of our wits. I dropped the bulb and let go of the ladder, screaming in shocked surprise. Donald started yelling as the ladder wobbled and collapsed. He crashed onto the floor like the bungling giant in *Jack and the Beanstalk* amidst even more screams from MIL. Suzanna started screaming in her bed upstairs. Jojo the black mongrel next door who loved playing with my daughter started barking. This triggered off more barking and canine howls all over the neighbourhood.

"AIIYEEEE! You killed him. He's dead, my poor son is dead! Now you happy *lah*, become merry widow. Police, help! Call the police! Murder!" MIL screeched.

"OH SHUT UP, Mother!" retorted Donald as he picked himself up laboriously from the floor, extricating himself from the spindly ladder. His layers of fat probably protected him from a bad fall, I surmised, grateful for once.

MIL was even more shocked than if her son had died. He had never ever been rude to her in his entire life.

"Are you alright, Donald?" I asked worriedly.

"Yeah, no broken bones. Now, if you please, let me try again, one more time."

MIL charged forward, nudged me aside and grabbed hold of the dented ladder.

"*Mari, gua pegang*. You can trust me, son, I will hold the ladder with all my life."

I left them in the kitchen fussing away over the light bulb. I ran upstairs, grabbed my suitcase from under the bed and threw in a whole pile of clothes. Gently taking Suzanna by the hand, we crept down the stairs, out of the house and into the car. I started the engine, glided down the driveway and sped away towards my mother's home. I had had enough. This was the very last straw.

I'm not the type who will threaten people with ultimatums. I'm just not the either-you're-with-me-or-against-me kind of person. Especially when it's a choice between one's wife and mother. Of course, a son has to take care of his mother. But for sanity's sake, I cannot stay under the same roof as MIL.

I tell Donald I'd like to be a weekend wife, just visit me and our daughter during weekends and the rest of the week stay with your mother. He doesn't even need to pay for my lodging. I'm doing very well in my job and with the recent promotion, I've been given a huge pay hike and a generous housing allowance. Donald is absolutely torn between his mother and me and has been begging me to return home, but I'm not ready. Not yet.

My life is serene again, no more jangled nerves bordering on a nervous breakdown. I'm glad the light bulb blew, no more darkness, only a lightness of being.

Macam Ah Pek kalah judi
Translation – like old Uncle who's lost money gambling
Meaning- Someone who looks tired and sad.

Manek cheroot cases
(Images courtesy Ken Yap)

Mosquito net holder
(Image courtesy the Peranakan Museum, Singapore)

An assortment of nyonyaware, blue and white nyonya plates,
glassware and crockery from Britain

Through Lara's Eyes

In the early hours of the morning, all was silent and hushed on Clove Lane, a row of eighteen colonial houses wedged in the heart of busy, bustling Kuala Lumpur in the 1980s. Office blocks, shopping complexes and high-rise apartments sprouted up in what was known as the "Golden Triangle" nearby, but this row of prewar houses with its unique 1900s architecture had eluded the developers' wrecking ball, snug and secure in its history of three generations living there.

Lara Lee, 25 years old, belonged to the third generation. Her late grandparents had bought a house at Clove Lane for seven thousand ringgit, a princely sum at the turn of the 20th century, and moved here in 1913. Lara's father was born here. When he married after World War II, he brought his bride to live with his parents and raised his family here – two daughters and a son. Lara, the second daughter, slept in the front room upstairs with her sister, her brother occupied the middle room and her parents the room at the back overlooking an open courtyard.

It was still dark and dewy, even the birds had not started their birdsong. The peace was broken by the sudden ringing of the telephone downstairs in the second hall. Lara jumped out of deep sleep, startled. She groaned, hoping it would shut up but it went on, jarring, persistent. Ignore, go back to sleep, she contemplated, but it might be important. Reluctantly, she fumbled out of bed, ran down the steep wooden staircase with its twenty-two steps and picked up the phone.

"Hello?"

"Help! My dad has fallen off his bed. Please, can your father come over and help us get dad back into bed?"

The call was from Hui Ning, her neighbour who lived directly across the road. Both their fathers had grown up at Clove Lane, close friends since childhood. Lara's father, Mr Lee had turned sixty and was fit, strong and healthy but Hui Ning's father, Mr Soh, suffering from lung cancer, had been given only a few months to live. His wife, Mrs Soh, who liked to come over and chat with her good friend, Mrs Lee, had confided her fears and anxieties to the Lees a few weeks ago. Mr Lee had told her to call if she or her family needed help.

When Mr Soh fell that morning, the Sohs made that call.

"Papa! Uncle Soh fell off his bed. They need your help," Lara yelled from the courtyard to her father in the room above.

Her father mumbled something incoherent, still half-asleep.

In a few minutes, her father came storming down the stairs. He had changed into his usual black pants and Pagoda T-shirt. He always had a cup of coffee before he stepped out but today, he charged out of the house without saying a word, not pausing to have a drink, nor even to catch his breath. Lara caught a glimpse of his face and then he was gone.

Lara helped hasten her father's exit by unlocking all the doors – the grill door with its heavy padlock, the bolts of the thick wooden door and the gate. She watched her father dash across the street and disappear into the house opposite. Lara turned back into her house, looking forward to crawling back into bed. She left the gate and door open, confident he would be back in a short while.

Her mother came downstairs, still in her night sarong and cotton top, "What's happened, Lara?"

"The neighbours opposite called. They need Pa's help to get Uncle Soh back into bed. He fell."

"Oh," Ma looked troubled, "Tell your Pa not to lift anything heavy, he has a bad back. Quickly, run over and caution him."

An intense sense of foreboding came over Lara, a feeling that that was not going to be a normal day and something terrible was about to happen.

As if on cue, a piercing scream rang across the street, gripping Lara and her mother, turning their blood icy-cold. Dogs barked and one by one, lights were switched on. No one could recall such a bloodcurdling scream or anyone ever screaming in such terror at all on Clove Lane – it was a relatively peaceful and harmonious street of close-knit families and friends. The scream came from the direction of the Sohs.

Lara dropped everything – keys, padlocks – and ran

with all her might towards the neighbour's house. She felt as if she were running in a dense, swirling fog, smothering, dragging her down, screams reverberating in her head. She pleaded, "Please, Papa. Please, say you're alright."

The door at the Soh house was wide open, with no one downstairs and noises, running and commotion upstairs. Lara scrambled up the steep stairs into the front room. She was horrified to see her father on the floor beside Mr Soh's bed. Uncle Soh was back in bed, eyes closed, breathing heavily. Hui Ning stood beside the bed, between the two men, looked petrified.

"Lara, your father helped put my dad back into bed, then... then he just collapsed! My mum's calling for an ambulance now," she gasped.

Lara knelt down beside her father. He lay motionless, his eyes staring straight ahead.

'Papa, Papa, are you alright? Papa!'

No answer, not a quiver of recognition. She put a small pillow under his head to make him more comfortable.

Just then a shriek from Uncle Soh's wife who had come back into the room and was watching her husband.

Uncle Soh's loud, raspy breathing had suddenly stopped. His wife grappled with the bedsheets and blankets, struggling to find his pulse on his right hand.

"Oh, he's gone... he's passed away," she sobbed.

"Come here, all of you, come and say goodbye to your father," she wailed to her children.

At the same time, Lara kneeling beside her father, saw

her father's eyes looking glazed at her, then roll upwards. She was not aware her father had passed away. She kept calling him, trying to revive him.

Lara's mother and brother reached the room, fear and worry all over their faces.

"Is Pa okay? What's happened?" her mother took in the devastating scene and gasped with horror at her husband sprawled, immobile on the floor.

"He's fainted, Mama," Lara tried to assure her.

"The ambulance should be here soon," Hui Ning tried to soothe.

Lara's mother swiftly instructed Lara, "Go back to the house, quickly gather some of Pa's things for the hospital."

Lara rushed home and started packing – a change of clothes, Pa's checked sarong, his red toothbrush, comb, towel, a novel by Han Suyin, one of his favourite authors sitting on his bedside table. Memories of happier times when she helped him pack for Port Dickson entered her mind. He loved that place, would he be able to return to Port Dickson? It would kill him if he couldn't.

He must have fainted running over like that, lifting up Uncle Soh and carrying him back into bed. Maybe it was more serious, maybe it was a mild stroke. What if it was worse? What if he had fallen into a coma?

But this was her Papa – six foot tall and strong, reliable, always there for them. He will be alright, he will recover. He will.

The ambulance arrived twenty minutes late. Lara prayed it would take her father to hospital without further delay. She waited outside impatiently with Papa's things in a small canvas bag. She saw the ambulance personnel come out of the Sohs' house with her father lying on the stretcher. But something was wrong. They were not carrying him into the ambulance, they were bringing him back towards his house! "What are you doing?" she cried.

"Quick! Get him to hospital, don't waste any more time!" she begged even as her heart began to tighten in an unbearable knot.

One of them, a kind Malay man, muttered uncomfortably, "I'm sorry. But he's dead."

"Dead? How could he be dead? He was fine a few minutes ago. He's unconscious. *Pengsan saja*. Take him to the hospital, hurry!" Lara pleaded as tears flowed down her face.

"The ends of his fingers have turned stiff and blue, Miss. His body is cold. It's too late. He's gone. *Dia dah mati*."

Both of them shook their heads sadly.

"...really sorry, there's nothing we can do anymore," the other man said.

The ambulance men brought her father home. Lara, her sister and brother were in shock and disbelief. Lara's mother, holding her emotions in check, pointed mechanically to the men to place her husband's body on the *barleh*, the black mahogany bench used for afternoon naps for anyone too lazy to climb up the steep stairs to the bedrooms.

Her mother displayed an inner fortitude and strength. There was much to do – black mourning garb to put on, phone calls to make, relatives to inform, funeral arrangements, undertakers to call, obituaries to place in the newspapers. She told her daughters to cover the mirrors with white mahjong paper as was the custom and her son to light white candles at the altar. Then she attended to her husband's dead body, to wash him and change him into formal clothes with the help of a neighbour at Clove Lane.

"You are my favourite flower, Lara. You, your sister and your mother are my favourite flowers." I remembered my father's reply when I asked him what his favourite flowers were. I was only ten years old then, on a picnic, collecting a pile of lovely, dewy frangipanis scattered on the ground with my sister. Papa took us out to nature spots often, to parks, streams, waterfalls, to Bukit Blachan, Templer's Park, Kanching Falls, Lake Gardens, Fraser's Hill, sometimes just up to The Gap for chicken chop or Hailam mee. He loved his food.

It was the seaside resort of Port Dickson (also known as PD) he loved the most. Every school holiday, he would take us on a ten-day vacation to PD, two hours' drive away. It wasn't ruined by overdevelopment and commercialisation then, but was a charming, laidback town. The British company Papa worked for owned a property at Third Mile – two small chalets at the top of a small hill separated from a beautiful white beach by the coastal road.

The chalet was basic: a lounge, two bedrooms, a dining room, kitchen and verandah with a speckled green marble bench facing the sea. Whenever we packed for PD, it was like moving house. Mama would bring along the whole works for cooking meals – sugar, salt, cooking oil, sauces, rice, food, along with our clothes, swimming gear, games, books, spades and pails. Papa's trusty Hillman would be packed to the hilt, blankets, pillows, bolsters inside the car and the rest of the paraphernalia filling up the entire boot.

Papa was happiest in PD. He loved the sea and spent hours sitting on the sea wall, watching its many moods: shimmering in the sun, windswept and choppy in wild weather, aglow in vermilion sunsets over the Straits of Malacca, brooding and mysterious under moonlit skies. Like Papa, we enjoyed watching the waves come rolling in on stormy days, roaring in awesome fury. I loved watching a storm unfold on the horizon – vertical streaks of grey awash like a Chinese brush painting covering half the sky with the other still cheery. The streaks turned ominous, blotting out more and more, the sea grew angrier, the air moist and heavy, the winds stronger and as the darkening stripes raced across the horizon, we would run home to the chalet, squealing with laughter as huge drops of rain pelted down.

At low tide, the sea would ebb far out leaving a swathe of sand banks, rocky and muddy patches, sections of knee-deep wading water and purple-green water under which seaweeds swayed. Papa taught us to wade through with no fear to reach the glittering sandbank where the waves crested and broke onto the wave-patterned sand. We played in the waves to our hearts' content, careful to head home once the tide turned and the sandbanks started shrinking.

The lone island in the bay, within walking distance during low tide, was our playground. We liked exploring the deserted island, collecting shells, racing hermit crabs, playing in the rock pools, watching goggle-eyed brownish mudskippers scurry across the mud. We grew accustomed to the sounds of the mangrove forest – the glurps, gloops, ticks and tocks as the twisted aerial roots belched and grumbled. Resting on boulders on the edge of our island, waves lapping all around, we watched passing ships on the horizon and tried to imagine the world beyond.

The bay was bordered by giant boulders and a cave on its far right. Pa loved to pull our leg, telling us stories of Ali Baba and the Forty Thieves, that if we uttered "Open Sesame" with conviction, the cave would open with fabulous treasures within. The walk to the cave was enchanting, passing by beach cottages with gardens of colourful bougainvillea, a derelict haunted bungalow and a grand mansion with its own beach pavilion on barnacle-encrusted cement stilts built right out to sea. Past a cliff covered with shrubbery and a stream cascading into a waterfall, Papa would point out monkey cups, carnivorous plants which preyed on unwary insects. Occasionally he would stop to observe brilliant-blue kingfishers settling on beached drift wood or signal upwards to gaze at eagles whirling majestically on the wind currents above. He taught us to love and respect nature, not to stomp on the skinny little pink crabs scuttling across the sands which always outran us anyway.

Papa enjoyed the simple pleasures of life. Going crabbing was one of them. On moonless nights when the tide was low, Hamzah, the jovial caretaker, would take us out crabbing. What fun wading in the shallows, clinging on to our carbide lamps and torches, straining our eyes for the silent, speedy crustaceans. Once we spotted one slinking along the bottom, we'd have to deftly slam the aluminium conical device around the crab trapping it in a steel prison, then pick it up and toss it into a pail.

Papa's hobby was going fishing with the pukat jala, a round fishing net with a metal chain trimming its entire edge. He would spend hours out in the sun and return with a bountiful catch. Mama would prepare the day's catch for dinner – the fish tasted amazing, fried to a delicious crisp. Mama didn't like the sun much, preferring to stay at the chalet, cooking delicious meals for us, down to goreng pisang or cucuk bawang for tea-time and delicious apom balik stuffed with banana slices for supper.

An enjoyable pastime was to drive to PD town after dinner, do some grocery shopping, sit by the esplanade and watch the boats bobbing in the water and fishermen preparing to go out to sea. As it got darker, the beams of the lighthouse at Cape Rachado pierced the sky, warning sailors of treacherous rocks and a deadly whirlpool. Mama loved to sing as we enjoyed balmy breezy nights at the esplanade. A song my father especially loved was:

> When the sun goes down
> And stars peep through
> When the sun goes down
> I think of you
> Of all the breezes
> The most I miss is
> Just one of your kisses
> When the sun goes down

This love for PD extended right up to young adulthood, when my university friends joined us. Those were wonderful times swimming, going for long walks, playing games and at night, out came the guitar and we'd have singing sessions. Each trip ended with a grand finale – a bonfire with roasted sweet potatoes, sugarcane, corn and a roast chicken. We lay on the poncho and gazed at the night sky, studded with millions of stars. Falling stars dropped too fast for wishes and shooting stars streaked by occasionally. We were young and idealistic and spent hours discussing God, creation, evolution, religion, politics, extra-terrestrial civilisations, UFOs, what we wanted to do with our lives. We couldn't wait to graduate, we thought we could change the world then.

Papa never lectured or told us what life would hold in store, allowing us to hold on to our dreams a little longer. He joined in our games, our songs, enjoyed our youthful company and long sojourns by the sea. He and Mama liked chatting with the kampong folks in the evenings when she carved out 'lidi' from coconut fronds as a pastime to make 'lidi' brooms. He relished Mama's delicious cooking and her company. It seemed as if there was nothing more he needed to complete his happiness. In a sense, I felt he was rich beyond compare, richer than many of his contemporaries, than others who owned far more wealth and material possessions.

Just two months before that fateful morning, Lara's parents had made several trips to visit his folks in his hometown of Malacca and her mother's relatives in Penang and Singapore.

Lara's mother commented it was odd that Lara's father had insisted on visiting as many members of the clan as possible, going to great lengths to get their contact numbers and addresses.

"And you know what else, Lara?" she added, looking a bit embarrassed, "your Pa said the strangest thing as we were coming home."

"What? What did he say?" asked Lara, curious, as her father, a man of few words, usually let her mother do all the talking.

"He told me, 'If I could live my life all over again, you are still the one I would want to marry, the one I want to live my whole life with all over again.' Weird, huh? He seldom expresses his feelings."

Lara teased her mother, "Waah, Papa said that? That's really something, Mama! How many men want to be with the same woman all over again? Most men can't wait to have someone totally new for a change!"

A shy, hesitant smile lit up her mother's face, but also a shadow of a worry, a feeling of inexplicable dread when peculiar things happen.

The ambulance drove slowly down Clove Lane and disappeared round the corner. A few hours later, the undertakers arrived. They parked in front of the houses of the Soh and Lee families. Out of one hearse, a glossy wooden coffin was brought into the Lee house, from the other, a heavy timber coffin into the Sohs'. Awnings were put up in front of both houses for the wake services. Stretching right across the road, they merged into one large roof linking the two households in mourning. A pair of white lanterns at each entrance announced a death in the family.

Events moved forward inexorably. At Lara's home, the undertakers placed Mr Lee's body from the *barleh* into the coffin. Cries of grief, sobbing and weeping began to ring out as relatives and friends grieved over the loss of a much beloved man.

The late Uncle Soh's widow came over with some relatives to pay their last respects to Mr. Lee. Sobbing, heartbroken for the bereaved Lee family, she told Mrs Lee, "I'm sorry... really sorry... I didn't know... didn't know he had a heart problem... we wouldn't have made that phone call... I don't know what to say, no words to express my regret, please forgive me..."

Everyone waited, wondering how Mrs Lee would respond. Despite her devastating loss and pain, she found the strength to transcend casting blame.

She reached out to Mrs Soh, hugged her and assured her it wasn't her fault. She was not to bear that burden, no one expected this to happen. They wept in each other's arms, two friends who became widowed at the very same instant.

As more people poured into the Lee household to pay their last respects, Lara noticed a peon in a shabby brown uniform and a young dispatch boy from her father's office, weeping by the coffin, visibly distraught, touching her father's hands respectfully, blessing him. Kumar, the peon, spoke in Malay to Lara.

"The whole office heard this terrible news. I had to come to say goodbye to him. Your father was a very good man, a very kind person. Always helping people, especially the poor, always lending me money because I was often in debt. He never turned people in need away. And now, see, even his last breath he is helping someone. Bless him, bless his soul."

In the afternoon, the beggar who came once a month to our house to collect his 'allowance' from Lara's father called out for Mr Lee. The funereal symbols, the ghostly lanterns and the bereaved family of his benefactor shocked him into silent grieving and expressions of deep respect. He walked away down the old street of pre-war houses, his shoulders stooped.

Papa did have a chance to get out of Clove Lane, I remember. This was when the Bangsar residential estate was being developed in the mid-1970s and Papa's sister tried to persuade him to join her in her move to Bangsar. She had booked three houses and wanted to pass one to her brother. Papa gave all sorts of excuses: too expensive, too far away from the children's schools, their parents won't be able to adapt, too many good friends and neighbours to leave behind. Truth

was, he enjoyed life at Clove Lane and probably had no plans to leave at all till the day he died.

Stepping on to Clove Lane feels like falling into a time warp, a forgotten feature from British colonial times. The double-storey houses, nine on each row, had short facades and long interiors comprising two halls and an inner courtyard. The walls were incredibly thick and the high ceilings kept the interiors cool. Each had its own verandah design with arches, balustrades, balconies and Roman pillars. Our house had blue, amber and green stained-glass windows, a solid red timber door and rustic-brown, indigo and orange floor Italian tiles which my Grandma from Malacca specially commissioned to give it a Straits Chinese flavour.

Like Pa's generation, the present generation at Clove Lane enjoyed the camaraderie and close friendship ties. No child was left out or lonely, everyone joined in the activities. Every evening, we would come out to play: the girls Five Stones, Hopskotch, Masak Masak, What's the time Mr Wolf, while the boys played Hide and Seek, cards, marbles, caught spiders, whacked each other at Chopping. The passing years saw a shift to badminton, ping pong, volleyball, cycling. The biggest excitement was when the younger generation and their fathers got together to play Rounders, everyone would come out to watch and cheer. During the May 13 race riots in 1969, when a curfew was imposed and schools were closed, this little street of eighteen houses was like a carnival, with the young out on the street playing, flying kites, hanging around, having a grand holiday.

During Chinese New Year, the driveways were covered ankle-deep in red paper, remnants of burnt out firecrackers and fireworks.

My Pa and Uncle Soh were the two biggest sponsors, buying home baskets of fireworks, firecrackers and sparklers for the children – and themselves – to play. On Chinese New Year's day, they put up long bamboo poles and strung up fearsome long rolls of firecrackers with a huge cluster at the end. Neighbours gathered around excitedly and watched as lion dance troupes pranced to the pulsating music of gongs, drums and cymbals. After the lion dancers had grabbed the ang pow strung high up on the pole with sprigs of lettuce, the show would end in a noisy climax of firecracker explosions, shrieks and laughter.

When the Mooncake Festival arrived, lanterns in rabbit, dragon, monkey, chicken, fish and rocket shapes and colourful Japanese lanterns were hung in the porches and gardens. The street looked beautiful all lit up at night in the soft glow of lanterns. The children, carrying their lanterns, would go for a walk round the neighbourhood while their parents chatted, sipped tea, enjoyed mooncakes under the full moon.

When vendors came by, this became an opportunity for residents of Clove Lane to catch up on gossip around the vendor's stalls. Papa liked to wait for the Yong Tau Foo man in the evening with his steaming hot tofu, springy fish balls, glistening red chillis stuffed with delicious fish paste. My sister and brother adored the ice cream man who came around on a bicycle, complete with a spinning wheel which you got to twirl and won prizes of more ice cream. My fondest memory has to be the Dim Sum man who came late at 11 pm. We would be in bed by then, not too keen to change out of our pyjamas and come down to the street. Grandma had her methods – lowering a wicker basket out of the window and hollering her orders. The vendor would fill it up, and up came the jaunty basket loaded with piping-hot barbecued pork buns and dim sum for supper.

Everyone at Clove Lane knew each other, from the architect, the optician, the dentist, the accountant, the hardware merchant, to the plumber, the portly car mechanic, the old albino lady who lived in a rented room, the shoe salesman, the grumpy mahjong player, the noodle seller selling Wan Tan noodles at the back of his house. My parents liked to relax on rattan chairs at the front of the house every evening after dinner and chat with neighbours who passed by. No one could have imagined that the fate of two families living there would intertwine in such a tragic way.

The 'problem' with Papa was he was a very kind man who never turned down a request for help. At his office, he was jokingly called Vampire because of his constant cajoling of his colleagues to donate blood along with him. When Mama cleared his drawer months after his death, she was astounded to find a box full of medals he had received for blood donation. He never told us, probably didn't think it was important.

I saw him in action firsthand helping people in distress. It was on a trip to Klang one Sunday afternoon – Papa loved the seafood at the restaurant by the Port Swettenham jetty. He was driving us towards Klang when we saw coming towards us in the opposite lane, a white car somersaulting over and over in a swirl of red dust till it rested turn-turtle on the divider. Immediately, Pa pulled his car to the side, told us to stay put, ran over to help the trapped passengers. With the help of several others, he pulled them out and got them into a car to head to the nearest hospital. He brought a bloodied, injured man across the road into our car and drove him *to the hospital in Klang. Papa's shirt and hands were covered in blood but it didn't bother him. He was pleased he was able to help.*

The two families decided separately on a two-night wake. Incense and the smoke of joss sticks and candles wafted over Clove Lane. Cars were jam-packed up to the adjoining streets, and passengers had to walk as there was no through road. Vans kept arriving delivering wreaths and bouquets of flowers. Mourners streamed in to pay their last respects, some confused and confounded by two houses in mourning simultaneously.

At the Sohs' house, Taoist priests in yellow robes chanted accompanied by gongs, cymbals and bells, paper possessions were burned to accompany the deceased on his journey. At Lara's house, Buddhist monks in saffron robes chanted sutras and dedicated them to Mr Lee. They comforted his grief-stricken wife and children and advised them not to grieve, he had gone on to another life, certainly a happy one. In the sonorous, lulling chants, Lara wept, missing her father deeply, her mother was inconsolable. His family and friends found it unbearably hard to accept his death.

After two days, one funeral procession left the street followed by the other. The awnings came down in the late afternoon, the lanterns, florescent lights, portable fans, electrical wiring, chairs and tables with white tablecloths were packed up and taken away. Life at Clove Lane gradually settled down into its usual pace, the absence of two beloved residents seared into its consciousness.

I was only 25 years old when I lost Papa. In my dreams of the future, he would be there, always a beloved and needed presence, laughing, beaming with happiness at all the milestones of our lives, he would be at my wedding yet to take place, he would enjoy his grandchildren yet to be born, he would travel with me in my future journeys.

We were taught if you do good deeds, you will be rewarded. So what kind of twisted karma was this that Papa should die helping someone? What cruel fate to be killed being a good Samaritan? But I am too much my Pa's daughter, he who found joy in the ocean's moods, star-studded skies, storms on the horizon, kingfishers and monkey cups, waterfalls and delicious food, so much to love in life and so little time. Choosing a path of negativity was not what he would expect from us. He would want us to live life the way he did, with kindness and compassion, reaping simple pleasures in return.

Thirty-five years later, I received a text message on my phone from my cousin. She said she was amazed when she hailed a taxi near Clove Lane and the taxi driver asked if she lived on that street. He told her about a kind and brave man who died while helping his friend at Clove Lane. My cousin told him she was a niece of that same man. The taxi driver was surprised at the serendipity,

then went on about the courage and selflessness of that gentleman.

He told her his own life was touched by that gentleman, Mr Lee. The taxi driver said he came from a poor background and could not find a job after secondary school. Mr Lee heard about the young man and got him a job at the British company where he worked. He even came to pick the unemployed youth from the low-cost flats, coached him and drove him to the interview. The youth worked as a dispatch boy and moved up through the company rank and file, eventually retiring comfortably. He now drove a taxi as a semi-retirement job. He told my cousin he was at her uncle's funeral at Clove Lane and remained deeply grateful to the kind and soft-spoken Mr Lee. I cried reading her messages. To think that Papa was still remembered in this way after all these years.

My thoughts drift to that tragic morning long ago. What if I hadn't answered that call? What if I had gone back upstairs and knocked gently on Papa's door? What if I hadn't yelled from downstairs and woken him up so suddenly? What if I had delayed him by making him a cup of coffee? Or unlocked each door slowly, or couldn't find the keys. What if, what if?

The only way to carry on is to let go of the baggage that chokes up your heart. I try to comfort myself that if he didn't go the way he did that morning, he would have died helping someone with his very last breath. My Papa.

I love this reindeer motif on my manek shoes because of the delightful fusion of east and west.

My father, sister and me, a few months old, at the verandah of my family home.

Picnicking with my paternal Grandpa.

A picnic at the Lake Gardens with my Papa and maternal Grandpa.

The boys who grew up on the same street as I, posing for a photo before a football game.

My sister and I serving tea to Grandpa.

My brother performing the seroja ceremony with our maternal Grandpa during Chinese New Year. My mother is in sarong kebaya.

We spent many happy times at the Harrisons and Crosfield chalets at Third Mile Port Dickson.

My favourite pair of manek shoes made by a skilled shoemaker. His skilled craftsmanship won him an UNESCO Award of Excellence for Handicrafts.

About the Author

Lee Su Kim is a Malaysian writer whose creative, literary and cultural activist endeavours and scholarly works have received considerable attention in Southeast Asia and internationally. Her light touches of humour, dry wit, sharp observations and fluid prose can be enjoyed in her three bestsellers – *Malaysian Flavours: Insights into Things Malaysian, Manglish: Malaysian English at its Wackiest* and *A Nyonya In Texas: Insights of a Straits Chinese Woman in the Lone Star State.*

Her first collection of short stories, *Kebaya Tales: Of Matriarchs, Maidens, Mistresses and Matchmakers,* is another bestseller and has been reprinted several times. In 2011, it was awarded the national Popular-Star Readers' Choice Awards (Fiction). Her second collection of stories, *Sarong Secrets : Of Love, Loss and Longing,* was published in 2014. *Manek Mischiefs : Of Patriarchs, Playboys and Paramours* completes her trilogy of short stories.

She was born in Kuala Lumpur to a baba from Malacca and a nyonya from Penang. Educated at the Bukit Bintang Girls' School, Kuala Lumpur, Su Kim holds a Bachelor of Arts in English, a Diploma and Masters in Education from the University of Malaya, Kuala Lumpur.

She lived in the US for four years and earned a Doctorate in Education from the University of Houston in 2001. Formerly Associate Professor at the School of Language Studies & Linguistics, Universiti Kebangsaan Malaysia, where she lectured and researched on language, culture and identity, she is now a full-time writer, educationist and language consultant.

She is the founding President of the Peranakan Baba Nyonya Association of Kuala Lumpur & Selangor, formed in 2008. She enjoys and shares cultural complexity beyond cuisine, *sarong kebaya* and *kasut manik* as a frequent presenter of the rich diversity of being nyonya. Her website is at www.leesukim.net. Follow her at www.facebook.com/ LeeSuKimAuthor.

Also by the author:

- *Malaysian Flavours: Insights into Things Malaysian*

- *Manglish: Malaysian English at its Wackiest*

- *A Nyonya In Texas: Insights of a Straits Chinese Woman in the Lone Star State*

- *Kebaya Tales:*
  Of Matriarchs, Maidens,
  Mistresses and Matchmakers

- *Sarong Secrets:*
  Of Love, Loss and Longing